Welcome to Gold Street

Samantha Clark

D1563070

Library of Congress Cataloging-in-Publication
Clark, Samantha, 1967-
 Welcome to Gold Street / Samantha Clark.
    pages cm
 ISBN 978-1-937240-54-7 (pbk. : alk. paper) -- ISBN 978-1-937240-55-4 (ebook : alk. paper) 1. Middle-aged women--Fiction. 2. Quilting shops--Fiction. 3. Ghosts--Fiction. 4. Albuquerque (N.M.)--Fiction. I. Title.

 PS3603.L36873W45 2015
 813'.6--dc23

                              2015009627

                              20150327
                        Casa de Snapdragon LLC
                         12901 Bryce Avenue, NE
                          Albuquerque, NM 87112
                          casadesnapdragon.com

                  Printed in the United States of America

Dedication

Thanks to the Sunshine office building for the best writing space in Albuquerque.

My gratitude to a pair of Legal Eagles and all of the Low Writers at El Chante: Casa de Cultura for nurturing my work.

Finally, this book wouldn't be possible without the support of my husband and daughter. All my love to Eric and Lynn.

CHAPTER 1

Summer

Nancy was sensible, practical, and didn't believe in foolishness.

So it was with shaking hands she dialed the number in the newspaper advertisement. The voice answering the phone sounded terribly young.

"Heather."

Nancy waited for some type of greeting—a Hello? or May I help you? The silence was deadening. She took a deep breath and plowed ahead with a trembling voice.

"Um, I'm calling about the for rent ad."

"Okay." Silence again.

Was everyone here this rude? She wondered if she was making a mistake.

"Is the retail space still available?"

"Which one?"

Nancy glanced around the city block. Gold Street wasn't love at first sight. She longed for greenery like back home. She grimaced at the never-ending brown dirt and concrete of the Southwest. Two stunted trees stood in the middle of the sidewalk providing little shade. She gulped the thin high desert air trying in vain to calm the butterflies churning in her stomach. Looking around she found the numbers printed above the door.

"203 Gold Street."

"Yes, that's still vacant. What kind of business do you own?"

"I don't have one… at least not yet."

"Okay. So how were you planning to use the space?"

Nancy was flustered. Her face went deep red in blush, which only intensified the harsh midday sun. "I'm planning to open a store here in Albuquerque."

Heather's voice was not encouraging. "Have you ever owned a business before?"

"Er, no."

Suddenly Nancy was deeply embarrassed. It never occurred to her someone would ask her about her business experience, or lack thereof, while answering a real estate ad. Nor was she making any progress in finding out how much the rent cost.

She tried to clear her mind by looking around at the other stores on the street. Somehow all of them managed to open a business.

"Ma'am?" asked Heather.

Nancy took a deep breath to buck up her courage. This was going to be a lot harder than she planned. "Look, I'm brand new to town. I just got here, but driving around, I saw a bunch of vacant signs. Don't you need to find some renters?" Sweat began to trickle down her back in rivulets, soaking through her rumpled shirt. Was she going to pass out in the heat of the desert sun? She felt faint.

"Ma'am, I'm located around the corner from Gold Street in the Sunshine Building. If you're there I can meet you at the space in two minutes."

Nancy reluctantly agreed, but as she turned off her cell phone, she was ready to bolt. She had approximately one-hundred and twenty seconds to run away. Was she crazy for moving out West, like her ex-husband back in Indiana, said?

It wasn't too late for her to tuck her tail between her legs and run back home. Well, technically, she no longer had a home. She'd sold her house and most of her possessions. However, most folks got rid of their stuff when they retired anyway. She could always find a condo or RV.

She slowly started to edge down the street.

Was she overly tired from the stress and worry of throwing herself head-long into a new life, at her age? She paused to glance into the window of a storefront. A picture faintly flickered on and off the computer monitor on a desk. She tried to adjust her eyes to the glare from the harsh sunshine. She attempted to ignore the image, but the screen was too compelling. It was like a magical sign from the heavens above. The blinking computer light filled the otherwise dim room.

"Well, hello!"

Nancy jumped back in surprise. Next to the front door, with a key in her hand, was a tall beautiful woman with gorgeous brunette hair. A large smile lit up her radiant face. Nancy wondered if she'd been the homecoming queen two decades earlier. She read the sign painted along the window — Cosmic Travel & Tour Co.

"I'm Jane and I own this travel company. Welcome."

Jane chatted enthusiastically as she inquired about Nancy. In no time a younger woman appeared who Jane introduced as Heather. Nancy couldn't explain why, but something about Jane made her more uneasy. She never did trust a person who was too friendly or loose in the lips, despite Jane's beautiful appearance. Something about her wasn't quite right. She didn't give it too much more thought because of the pressing issue of dealing with finding a space for her dream of opening a quilting shop.

Nancy turned to the young woman twirling the ends of her long blond hair. Heather motioned to her to start walking back up the street as she began to explain the rates and terms of a lease. Jane followed along behind.

"Oh my, that's expensive," said Nancy. She was hoping to find cheap space so she would have plenty of money left over to purchase inventory. Rents in Indiana were quite a bit lower.

As soon as Jane saw the worried look on Nancy's face she launched into a monologue about how affordable Downtown was compared to similar neighborhoods around town. Did she know how much locating near the university or trendy Nob Hill would cost? Would she want her precious store in a generic strip mall? Nancy admitted she liked the idea of an old-fashioned main street with people walking around. As a quilter she liked traditional Victorian architecture with some history to it. She wasn't sure she could get used to the adobe buildings of Albuquerque, which seemed to ~~all seemed~~ to look the same, in the Pueblo-style neighborhoods of Old Town or Corrales. One vacation in Santa Fe years ago she was forever getting lost among the winding roads and brown buildings. Downtown felt easier to navigate, more like the buildings back home.

Heather opened the front door of 203 Gold. Nancy tentatively surveyed the store. It would need a lot of work. She frowned. It was more money out the door. Should she keep searching for a new location?

Then it happened. Heather, young enough to be her granddaughter, started to lecture Nancy in the same annoying tone her ex-husband used. Both of them seemed to doubt her ability to run a business. Heather's words became kindling, which started a fire deep inside Nancy. She got angry.

"Look here, young lady, I have been taking care of myself many years before you were born! I have the money to pay the deposits. I understand the terms of the lease and know I owe rent for all five years, regardless if I stay open or not. My credit is excellent. You don't have a good reason to deny me the space. How can you predict who will be successful? What makes you think I am going to be any less successful than any other store on this street?"

As Nancy paused for air, Jane jumped into the fray. She lectured Heather about not discriminating and threw in some additional comments about her Uncle George, who apparently owned the real estate company. As a bystander Nancy found Jane's personal attacks against the realtors in poor taste, except the nasty comments seemed to get the job done.

Heather threw up her hands in defeat. "Fine. You can sign a lease this afternoon."

Nancy still wasn't sure she wanted to stay, but now she was committed. Heather stalked off while Nancy and Jane walked back over to the travel company.

"What exciting news. You're going to have a quilt shop."

"Yeah, I had been thinking I should visit some other cities, like maybe Denver, before deciding." The panic was returning as her anger wore off.

"Let me know if you want to take a trip. I'm very good at cosmic tours. You're going to be happy on Gold Street. We all have special gifts. I'm sure you're going to discover yours. I see your aura is a deep red. I can feel strong flash of white energy in you."

Nancy winced at the last words. She didn't want an explanation from Jane about what the auras meant. It confirmed her suspicion a safe distance should be kept from Jane. She was relieved when Jane was interrupted by a phone ringing inside the travel company. As Jane disappeared into a back room Nancy was ready to leave the street. What had she gotten herself into? Was she supposed to find a lawyer or something before signing a lease? Once again she was overwhelmed by the enormity of the tasks at hand.

Still, she stayed put.

She knew she should go in search for shade from the brutal sun and a bottle of water.

Why couldn't she walk away from this peculiar store? Try as she might she still couldn't bring herself to move away from the glass. A beeping noise from inside caught her attention. The flicker of the computer monitor once again flashed the picture. It was the same as earlier — a quilt.

What an odd screen saver, she remarked to herself. She put her hand up to her forehead to lean closer to the window for a better look. Something was eerily familiar about it. She racked her brain trying to figure it out.

Wait a minute.

The plaid squares were the very same design she once made many years ago.

How could that be?

She started to remember her old quilt in detail. It had been assembled by a group of friends out of old high school dresses. She could still picture the plaid of her dress, the one that made her look like the model Jean Shrimpton, although perhaps a couple sizes larger. She bought the dress with her high school babysitting money, a modern fabric of wrinkle-resistant polyester that required no ironing. She was so mod back then, much to her mother's dismay.

A nicely dressed woman, coming out of the tea shop across the street, interrupted Nancy's memories. She wondered if someone would yell at, or at least question her, but the woman said nothing. She merely inspected Nancy from a distance then returned through the door. Did Nancy imagine she smiled?

The beeping inside the travel company become louder, forcing her attention back to the screen. The quilt was replaced by a video. Did the company broadcast travel ads?

She flattened her face against the window pane to get the best view possible. The video began to change. The camera rolled down country roads. She gasped at the scene in wonder. They were the roads of her small college town in Indiana! She recognized some of the landmarks. A big red barn marked the city limits. Nearby, Rick's Auto Repair did a brisk business. Was there a classic auto show in town? She couldn't recall the last time she saw the place busy.

She studied the cars on the lot. Among the oldies but goodies, she picked out a brown Chevy Impala just like the one her parents used to own. Next to it stood a baby blue Mercury Cougar, like the car her in-laws once owned. Further back sat a souped-up orange Ford Torino with black racing stripes. Her husband Bobby always wanted one, although he never bought it. What they owned sat in the very back—a dented black Dodge Dart. It was already old when they bought it, constantly broke down, and she never liked the jalopy. Funny, seeing the car now brought a wave of nostalgia.

The video moved down the street, passing the Roller Dome indoor skating rink and Sambo's restaurant. She pictured the food inside the coffee shop. Her favorite plate was the Mama Mumbo

Special—eggs any way you liked, along with a huge stack of pancakes. Well, she ate there regularly until she joined with others from the university to protest their racist images. Boy, that was years ago. Who would open a restaurant like that now?

The skating rink and Sambo's disappeared years ago. Over time some locals tried to make a go of the abandoned restaurant, but nothing seemed to stick. As the population of the area decreased, those buildings were torn down. How many years had it been since she saw the skating rink sign's flashing yellow bulbs announce the next town skate party?

Was this a historic video of Indiana?

That couldn't be her old street, the one where she and Bobby actually lived, right after they got married. The video floated past a row of parked cars, right up to the apartment building's front door. In later years the building would deteriorate, ugly colors of paint peeling in strips and fill with down-on-their-luck tenants. But when they first moved in, the contemporary design was innovative, with sharp lines and exposed natural wood panels.

Nancy never liked modern architecture, but she liked the skylights in this place. However, she never questioned Bobby's choice when he signed the lease. She couldn't remember them ever discussing where they'd live. He simply surprised her one day with a set of keys before their honeymoon. Until then, they shared a house with roommates. She enjoyed communal living, but people don't do that kind of thing once they're married, do they? Graduating from college meant growing up, right?

She couldn't tear her eyes away as the scene unfolded in front of her. The camera traveled up the walk to their front door. The complex was only a couple years old then with modern conveniences, such as a Dyna-Vac central vacuuming system. Bobby declared Nancy would never need to lug a vacuum cleaner around the apartment. Instead, she plugged in a hose and flipped a switch on the wall. That was the theory anyway. She recalled that the system often got clogged.

She became engrossed in the video and lost all sense of time and place, the way a person watching a movie loses track of the surrounding room. She felt like she was actually there.

CHAPTER 2

The apartment door opened directly into their living room, with harvest gold shag carpet. Someone left the shag carpet rake by the coat closet, ready for the almost daily task of fluffing to keep the carpet pretty. New furniture from J.C. Penney occupied the center of the room, while Nancy's beloved terrarium sat against the wall under the skylight. Nearby, her collection of glass jars for brewing herbal sun tea and starting sprouts sat on the window sill. Several house plants were dispersed throughout the room.

The stereo lid sat open, ready for a record album; the needle left half-hazard on the turn table. Bobby would be upset. He just bought an expensive diamond needle tip. Next to the stereo sat shelves made from pieces of lumber stacked across cement blocks. Records competed for space with the stacks of books. Her favorite paperback, Jonathan Livingston Seagull, sat open on the top of a pile to mark her page.

She was drawn to the sound of a radio playing down the hallway. She listened to the vaguely familiar local radio program in the distance.

"Hi cats, this is Blazin Bill with your top twenty countdown for the week of August Fourth, nineteen seventy-two. How are you enjoying this Friday? Are you mellow? Far out, because we only have four songs left until we get to the number one song in the country this week. Don't go away, we'll be right back."

Nancy tried to make out the muffled voice of someone talking in the kitchen as a radio ad came on. What was she doing in her old apartment? She stared at the afghan, crocheted in bright shades of orange, green and brown, draped across the back of the couch. Her grandmother patiently spent months making it for a wedding present.

"Here's number five, ladies and gents," blared the radio, mixed with a bit of static. "Our next song is for people who've ever been in love, to the max! I hear that. Get ready to groove to the smooth beat of Al Green."

Soft music drifted down the hallway from Green's "I'm Still in Love with You".

The doorbell rang, completely startling Nancy. She wasn't prepared for what happened next. In walked herself, but four decades younger. Nancy stared at herself in wonder.

Was she really that beautiful? She didn't recall ever feeling pretty. Look at how long and lush her hair was. Could that have really been her?

Are we ever the same people we used to be?

Nancy watched herself. Everything was so easy back then.

Except maybe it wasn't.

She saw the beautiful new outfit on the young Nancy. She had dressed up for the evening hoping Bobby would take her out to the Friday night movies, like when they were dating. She hoped to see Last Tango in Paris before it left the movie theaters. She would be so sad to miss it because it could be years before a much-edited version got played on late night T.V. However, at this point, she would sit through The Godfather or Deliverance if it got her out of the house.

She curled her long hair and carefully chose a silky multi-toned print maxidress. She spent extra time applying make-up, which she usually didn't wear much anymore, and painted her nails.

Nothing could hide the disappointment she was about to experience.

"Oh, hello, Pop Smith," the young Nancy said, as she opened the front door.

"You look swell there, Nancy." She gave him a smile. At least someone noticed her efforts.

"Didn't Bobby tell ya I was stopping by?"

"Um, no, sir."

"Not interrupting nothing, am I?"

She sighed and answered no. It was the truth.

"I see you gots everything set up here," as he politely glanced around the living room.

"Yeah, it's almost a month since our honeymoon and I'm still trying to get everything arranged. The spare room is full of presents that I still need to write thank you notes for. I have a red fondue set and I can't for the life of me recall who gave it to us."

"Nice clock over there on the wall," said Mr. Smith, as they both stopped to watch a silver sea gull float at the end of the second hand, as it went round and round a sky blue disc lined with silver balls instead of numbers. Nancy bought the clock because it reminded her of her favorite book. What was the saying, something about the sea gull who flies the highest can see the farthest? She looked around the room and wondered what her life now represented.

Mr. Smith quietly cleared his throat. He came over for a purpose, but she had no idea why. It would be rude to ask.

"Would you like some coffee or are you staying for dinner?"

Obviously she wouldn't go out anywhere anytime soon. She mentally searched her cupboards for a quick meal to fix. She had a box of instant rice and some pork chops in the fridge. She knew Mr. Smith would have no interest in the exotic tofu she found at the newly-opened specialty health food pantry, nor did he care for honey instead of sugar, her homemade yogurt, or the carob sesame bars she preferred for desserts.

He liked cooking typical for the area—which often included ground beef and a box of Velveeta cheese, and lots of desserts, such as salads made from Jell-O, canned fruit, whipped cream, and cream cheese or mini-marshmallows. None of her arguments convinced him to stay away from red meat or white sugar. He said it was un-American to eat hippie food.

"I'm off the phone," yelled Bobby from the kitchen. "Is Dad here yet?"

Nancy's cheeks flushed red as anger swelled up inside. Why didn't Bobby bother to tell her his father was coming for a visit?

Obviously they made plans without considering what she might want to do for the evening. This was just the kind of thing she and the other women discussed at a meeting on campus the other evening. They called it consciousness-raising. They were going to get the ERA — Equal Rights Amendment--passed. Soon it would be law; men must treat women as equals. Suddenly Nancy was conscious of a lot of things in her relationship with Bobby.

"Why don't you guys come back to the kitchen?" called out Bobby.

Nancy and Mr. Smith found Bobby at the table in his "Keep on Truckin" t-shirt with a couple of newspapers spread out. Why had she bothered with the nice contemporary white dinette set, from the Sears catalogue, with polyurethane-padded seats in avocado green, if he was just going to leave papers everywhere?

The radio caught everyone's attention. "This is Blazin Bill back again. I'm going to ask you a question — have you ever met a girl as fine as Brandy? I hear that. Brandy girl is some fine chick. Here at song number two is Looking Glass with…"

"Would you turn that off?" asked Nancy in annoyance.

"But we'll miss the number one song for this week."

"I can't stand that Bill guy. Why does he talk down to women? He shouldn't call an adult woman a girl on the air. Someone should make him stop."

"Why are you such a drag lately?"

Mr. Smith shifted uncomfortably from one foot to the other. He appeared to be at a loss for words. Bobby shifted the long antenna out of the way as he clicked the radio knob off.

"Here it is, Pops." Bobby pointed to the real estate section of the newspaper.

"So that's the one you kids are going to buy?"

"Yeah," said Bobby. "The ad here on the right is the one I told you we want."

"What are you talking about?" said Nancy, her voice climbing in pitch as she spoke. She didn't mean to get mad in front of her father-in-law, but it couldn't be helped. "We haven't discussed buying houses."

"Sure we did. Remember how my dad told us he would help us with the down payment after the wedding?"

"But I haven't looked at any properties."

"You don't have to. I've already found what we need, just like what we talked about. I'm getting you what you said you wanted."

"What I wanted was to be involved in the decision, not have someone else decide what I like!"

An angry silence filled the room.

"We're happy to get you kids a nice place," offered Mr. Smith. "Your mom and I just talked about how much we look forward to hearing the patter of some little feet around here."

"You didn't tell your dad?" She turned to face the older man, "I'm going to graduate school in the fall."

"Now whatever for?" asked Mr. Smith, in all sincerity. "You don't need to spend fool money on being over-educated in raising kids. Bad enough they got to eat that stuff that tastes like cardboard." He added under his breath, "Give them the pill and the ERA and they ain't female anymore."

"Look, Dad. It's fine for Nancy to get an advanced degree."

"You kids waited to get married," protested Mr. Smith. "Nancy isn't getting any younger."

Nancy mused over how thrilled Mrs. Smith had been about the wedding, only to be outdone by her own mother. Both families worried themselves sick over the two of them living in sin while undergraduates. Again and again her mother had asked--Why will he ever buy the cow when you give him the milk for free?

Once two people live together, it's time to get married, right? At the time, it wasn't a question. She couldn't really think of a better explanation of why they tied the knot. It's what people did.

"Besides," said Mr. Smith, "I thought you guys were against our fine young men doing their patriotic duty by serving our country."

"You can't blame that on Nancy, Pops."

"Any girl going to college takes the place of some fellow."

Ouch, Mr. Smith hit a nerve with Nancy. She and Bobby just talked about that subject. In the fall she would start a graduate teaching position, a year behind Bobby. The other day a group of friends smoked late into the night arguing about whether it was right to flunk a man, because he could lose his draft deferment and be shipped off to Vietnam. Nancy had generally agreed, until her consciousness-raising made her aware no one seemed concerned about the fate of women who weren't given the same opportunities as men.

Most of those guys would get back out of the service, and on the G.I. Bill to boot, but what kind of life were women condemned to live?

"If McGovern wins the fall election, we won't have to worry about it," said Bobby.

"Ha," said Mr. Smith. "Who would vote for that amnesty, abortion and acid pinko? Didn't you just see in the paper got rid of his running mate? That Eagleton guy needed shock therapy, for Christ's sake. What kind of man is that?"

"Look here, Dad," Bobby, pointed his finger to one of the newspaper pages. "A recent Time magazine poll found seventy-seven percent of respondents said Eagleton's medical record would not affect their vote."

"Nobody trusts a whack job."

"Oh, fooey," said Nancy. "Getting treatment for medical conditions should be encouraged. He's a role model for a new kind of man."

"He's your kind of guy?" Mr. Smith raised his eyebrows. "Look here, I don't care if you kids now have the vote everywhere in the country now. It still won't put McGovern in office. Nixon is a fine president. I don't know any of the brothers down at the hall who would vote for a left-wing extremist. They should have nominated a real man like Humphrey."

Until recently Mr. Smith was a life-long Democrat and union member down at the plant. He spent endless hours talking politics with the other fellows at the union hall. Who would have thought the day would come when he voted Republican?

"If Nixon is such a great guy, how come this came out in the paper?" Bobby dug out the student newspaper from the pile and flipped through the sections until he found a rumpled page. He read aloud, "The Washington Post reported this week—Bug Suspect Got Campaign Funds. In a detailed article the Post claimed a twenty-five thousand dollar cashier's check, from President Nixon's re-election campaign, was deposited back in April of this year into a bank account of one of five men later arrested at this summer's break-in at Democratic National Headquarters."

"You think that's going to stop Nixon?" asked an amused Mr. Smith.

The phone on the wall rang. Nancy grabbed the plastic handle and stretched the phone cord as far as it would reach out into the hallway, to avoid disturbing the conversation between the two men. When she finished, she noticed her father-in-law getting ready to leave.

"Thanks for the offer of dinner, but I promised your mom I would get home. I just wanted to stop by to see if you were ready to buy that place."

"Sure thing, Dad."

"I don't know about that," said Nancy. Bobby flashed her an annoyed look.

After he left, Bobby turned to face Nancy. "I don't know why everything I do for you is wrong. You used to be so happy."

"Yeah, that's been awhile..."

"Say, why don't we go over to Yoder's Café by the pond? We can hike around. On the way, I can show you the house I found. It's everything you said that you wanted. It's really old and everything. You've been talking about planting a huge garden and maybe raising animals, just like that Firefox book. I was going to surprise you. It's an old farm house past the new development on the edge of town."

"Maybe that's okay."

"There's a couple of apple trees and a creek that runs into a little pond. It's perfect."

She sat silent for a minute. "Look at what I'm wearing."

Bobby froze, and for the first time all evening, seemed to notice her fancy dress. "Well, what did you go and put that on for? We can't walk around the pond with you dressed like that. Go and change into your blue jeans."

As Nancy left to change as ordered, she began to wonder — why had she bothered?

****

"Excuse me, are you alright?"

Nancy pulled away from the Cosmic Travel & Tour Co. window to stand upright. She blinked her eyes several times to adjust to the bright New Mexico sun.

"I'm okay," she said to the concerned young woman standing in front of her, but was she?

"Do you need a drink of water? I have a water cooler over at my yoga studio next door."

"No, but thank you." Standing up straighter Nancy began to regain her composure. "Do you enjoy being located on here on Gold Street?"

"Oh, yes. I'm Rachel."

The woman described all the various benefits of being Downtown. As she continued to talk, Nancy couldn't help but think maybe the trip wasn't so hard, after all. Here was the fresh start she promised herself years ago.

CHAPTER 3

6 Months Later

Nancy sighed and shuffled a stack of bills around an antique table. The comforting aroma of freshly brewed tea did little to cheer her mood. She was down to ten dollars left in her bank account. Her inheritance and all of her retirement funds were gone. How was she going to pay the mortgage on the modest house she'd bought after arriving in town?

Fay gave Nancy a sympathetic nod and patted her arm. She smiled in her gentle manner, then quietly walked to the middle of the room to arrange a new display for her tea shop and gallery.

Nancy sat back and watched Fay's graceful work. From behind, Nancy could never guess Fay was already in her seventies. She carried herself in a regal Boston manner, and always dressed in a classic tailored style. Fay was the only person she knew who wore a Burberry trench coat in the bright Albuquerque winter sun without looking odd.

However, being odd wasn't a crime in Albuquerque. Since moving a few months ago, she noticed plenty of Albuquerqueans who marched to the beat of their own drums.

Wasn't this why she relocated from Indiana? She refused to spend her golden years in a dark, lonely house reading books and enduring harsh Midwestern winters. She was also afraid to become a snowbird flown south to an overheated retirement community in Arizona, as her parents had done. Here, she still felt as young forty. Since retiring, she actually felt even younger. She was ready to start an exciting new phase of life.

How had she run out of funds so quickly? Panic began to run through her veins. It was the first time in her adult life she'd completely run out of money. Beads of perspiration formed above her eyebrows.

She gathered her bills into a neat stack. Calculating cash flow never entered her blissful dreams of opening a quilt shop. Thinking about money wasn't how she planned to spend her days! It was a comfort she located next door to Fay. Nancy was drawn to the tea shop's robin's egg blue exterior with gold lettering.

Nancy watched Fay finish a divine shelf of white lace and delicate knick knacks. Fay's quaint shop looked like a boutique from a Parisian back alley. She admired Fay's artistic arrangements of sumptuous floral notecards, fountain pens, and glass paperweights. Fay rotated art shows every month on the walls.

Nancy wondered if Fay was blue blood by birth, or if she acquired her excellent tastes along the way. She probably never worried about money. Fay remarked about her husband, in a long ago life, back in Boston. He was a dashing surgeon with taste to rival Fay's. They made a handsome pair, throwing fancy parties in their exquisitely decorated home. Eventually, they divorced when he ran off with one of his nurses.

"Were you upset when he left you for a younger woman?" Nancy asked bluntly.

"Good heavens no," replied Fay, her head held aloft. "The nurse was a handsome young man. Dashing really, although horrible at entertaining."

Fay begrudged her husband more for disrupting their perfect world than for falling in love with a man.

"Really," remarked Fay in a moment of reflection, "why couldn't he just go about his business in a quiet and respectful way? Most middle age men carry on a private life. Why tear apart our family and make a public spectacle of his preferences?" she wondered aloud.

Nancy recalled they had children.

Fay added, "My mother always told me a decent lady or gentleman does not hang their underclothing outside on a wash line for the entire neighborhood's enjoyment. Privates should be tucked away inside the home, not flaunted."

Nancy nodded emphatically.

Nancy often stopped by Fay's Downtown Tea Shop & Gallery. Fay was a wonderful listener and always prepared a new variety of hot tea for her to sample. The aroma alone eased her rattled mind.

However, today Nancy noticed the differences between herself and Fay. Fay was the youngest of the Greatest Generation of the World War II era, while Nancy was one of the first Baby Boomers to retire. Despite the two women being less than a decade apart, she observed they came from separate worlds. It was more than different geographic histories.

Nancy could not imagine staying married to her former husband Bobby just to keep up appearances for their Indiana friends and neighbors. Her early 1970s consciousness-raising awakened her to the fact she needed more from life than a finely decorated doll house where she played housewife. Their little two acre farm outside of their university town, which some days resembled a commune, would never appear in a decorating magazine, like Fay's. Still, it was a cozy home she hated to sell, Not to mention she gave up the land she once used for one of her favorite passions — animal rescue.

Little did Nancy ever imagine she would never find an actual soul mate and partner to replace the hollow excuse of a marriage she experienced with Bobby, nor did raising children on her own ever enter the picture. Instead, she built a brilliant academic career.

One of the highlights of the days after her divorce was a quilting circle with her old friends from high school. They managed to stay in touch over the years, and she liked the bond of teamwork. Whenever life seemed to get the better of her, she remembered the women gathered together in her living room as they stitched a queen sized bed spread. She carried the quilt with her into each new romance. Each new stack of papers to grade, and each new novel she eagerly devoured were left on the quilt. Her cats would snuggle and sometimes scratch the floral patterns with their claws, but somehow the tattered quilt survived until a neurotic shepherd dog she rescued tore the stuffing out of the quilt to finally destroy it. Some days she wished she could go back, not only to make another quilt, but to find the younger woman who slowly disappeared.

She continued to quilt, although she never created anything as ambitious as her first hand-pieced quilt by her circle of friends. She now assembled quilts with a sewing machine. She stuck to smaller sizes she could snuggle up with on the couch or use for decoration, but even a twin sized bed spread, machine pieced, could take a couple years to finish by herself by hand.

Nancy laid the assembled fabric and center batting on a quilt frame. She then sat like a monastic scribe bent over a holy book, lost in the meditative up and down of the needle weaving in and out of the fabric. Up and down. Hand sewing created a peaceful rhythm in her head.

She enjoyed the creative aspect of quilting, and how random pieces of cloth assembled into a practical household item.

As an anthropology professor, Nancy studied and taught about the obscure history of women and quilting. It angered her to think how early 20th century painters got credit for creating Modernism in America while Amish quilters of all periods were ignored.

She harbored a deep respect for the pioneering women who stitched together old clothing scraps to help their families survive the winters.

She broke down crying once while holding a slave bed spread. Slave quilts are distinctive because of the irregular shapes of their patterns. When slave women assembled the little pieces of scrap cloth they found, they didn't possess large enough pieces of material to put together regular patterns of large squares or triangles. Instead, slave quilts were improvised, like a jazz music, with bits and pieces here and there. However the arranger could fit them together. The quilts were lessons in how to create something out of almost nothing.

"Don't you think?" asked Fay.

"Huh?" was the only answer Nancy gave. She suddenly remembered she was in Fay's store.

"You are a hundred miles away. I was remarking on the distinctive flavor of my new tea. Rather like a Vintage Earl Grey, don't you think?"

Nancy swirled the cold tea in a delicate bone china cup. She could no longer smell it because the steam was gone.

Looking at the cup reminded her of the pile of bills stacked neatly next to the saucer. She thought more about the differences between Fay and herself. If Fay were a quilt, she would be an American revolutionary pattern which took a decade to stitch, all finery that showed its wealth by elaborate detail.

Fay seemed to come from old money, although it was unlikely she would ever directly mention it. This included what Fay packed away in her underwear drawer of life.

Nancy would never ask such a blunt question anyway. Despite her recent move to the Southwest, she would always be a reticent Midwesterner at heart.

Nancy started to question the wisdom of moving to a new city and opening a quilt supply shop. She did her research in detail. She excelled at gathering background information, making analysis, and deriving insightful conclusions, all of which didn't seem to help with the problems of running a store.

"How does everyone else on the street stay open?" Nancy asked aloud, despite herself.

Fay sat down gently at the table. "Dear," she asked kindly, "are you having a bad day?"

Nancy sighed again. She needed to get out of her rut and adopt a more productive attitude.

Nancy turned to Fay and spoke to her directly for the first time all morning.

"I'm okay, Fay," she said as she watched the lifeless front door of her shop. "I just can't believe how much money opening a store really costs. I already spent my entire inheritance from my parents' estate in a few months, along with my own savings. I thought their nest egg would last me a couple years."

"Being broke is a temporary situation," admonished Fay. "Being poor is a state of mind."

Nancy drifted off again. She started to mentally go through the growing list of expensive things she didn't expect, such as the way moving the dividing wall in the front of the store in order to open up a display area triggered an entire remodel to meet new zoning codes. There were the added costs of stocking inventory and getting required certificates, inspections, and a business license, which delayed her grand opening. Still she needed to come up with money to spend on marketing to get customers through the door. She didn't know where to begin, other than reverting to the skill she knew best—teaching. She posted flyers all over the neighborhood to advertise a new quilting class in a couple weeks.

Somehow, in the beginning, she indulged the fantasy just putting up a sign would entice hordes of grateful quilters to stream through her shop, and searching through bolts of fabric and assorted sewing notions. Her street sign, which cost thousands of dollars, was professionally designed by a graphic designer at an expensive sign company, because it needed to be a certain size, and meet special zoning requirements—the details of which conflicted between a new city sector plan and the landlord's requirements in the lease. They required expensive metal sides for plastic letters, and they wanted the sign specially wired to the front of the building with timers which lit the sign between sundown and 10 PM, even when the store was closed. The electrician's work on the sign triggered another round of city inspections.

She first considered naming her business Nancy's Unique Quilting Supplies, but almost suffered a heart attack when she received estimates from the sign company about the cost of such an elaborate name. She already filed her forms with the city, county and state, so she couldn't change her business name at such a point without creating a new set of nightmares. Finally she decided the sign should simply read Nancy's Quilting. Hopefully customers would understand she sold supplies, not finished quilts. The shortened name violated her lease, but as long as the landlord didn't say anything, she wasn't about to mention it.

Wasn't freedom why she decided to open her own place? She was free to make her own decisions and listen to a boss; that was her theory, anyway.

Lighting the sign at night did not attract customers any more than her cheerful window displays during the day. She spent too many quiet days with her quilt shop cat, Tompkins, as he rested peacefully on her lap.

Fay shifted in her seat and waited politely for Nancy to pay attention.

"Well," stated Fay thoughtfully, "I don't think most of the stores make much." Fay continued to mull over Nancy's question about how the shops along the street made a profit. "Yes, dear," stated Fay more decisively, "nobody makes lots of money on Gold Street anymore. Except for maybe Stella's flamenco dance studio. Proof that evil is its own reward."

Stella and Fay didn't get along. Okay, that was an understatement. Stella was loud and dyed her hair flaming red, even though she was beyond a certain age in Fay's opinion. Stella argued with every business owner on the street in the most dramatic and theatrical way possible. Her fights with a restaurant across the street over unauthorized use of her parking lot were legendary. She forever came up with reasons why her rent was too high or shouldn't be paid and woe to the customer who didn't pay on time, the contractor who used cheap building materials, or the fire marshals and city inspectors unlucky enough to have her studio on their inspection lists.

Despite her abrasive nature, Stella was an astute business woman. She also set up her beloved niece, Theresa M, with a coffee shop next door to the dance studio.

"Theresa M still works banquets on some Saturday nights over at the Hyatt Regency Hotel. I don't think she makes enough money yet to cover her expenses, even with her Aunt Stella's help."

Nancy gazed out the window at the other stores. A "for rent" sign sat in the window of an empty storefront down the street from the tea shop and gallery.

"We don't see Jane often," Fay said. "I don't see how she keeps the Cosmic Travel & Tour Co. open. Unless..." Fay's voiced trailed off. "Unless she leaves her store because she leads tour groups to fascinating places, but I don't know. Maybe her husband is just well endowed."

Fay and Nancy let their minds wander to what type of endowment Jane's husband might possess, and how their lives would be different if they each stayed married to a husband—and his income. Perhaps neither would spend quite so much time in their stores. Jane certainly seemed to know of plenty of things to do other than tend shop.

"We don't see much of Rachel either," said Nancy. The Higher Power Yoga Studio sat dark most of the week, except for a few hours when Rachel held a class. Of course, the sign lit up at night like clockwork. Every sign on the street lit up after dark.

Fay explained Rachel worked at a local food co-op when she didn't teach. Being in her early thirties, never married, and trying to run her business herself, Rachel struggled most of any business on the street to stay afloat.

The business at the very end of the block was Marconi's restaurant. Carmen Marconi and her daughter Mary Ann both married, although their husbands' incomes didn't seem to lessen their workloads. They both spent every free moment at the restaurant. If they didn't cook, supervise, or serve, they bought ingredients and ordered tableware to replace the dishes which seemed to break every week.

Now Nancy thought about it more, she recalled Mrs. Marconi's husband died. She was only a little older than Fay, but seemed to be decades older. Maybe it was the cigarettes which etched deep lines into her face, or a lifetime of restaurant labor that left a stoop in her back. Nancy heard Mrs. Marconi's daughter was trying to get her to sell the business and retire.

Marconi's was a landmark in Downtown Albuquerque. During the 60s and 70s, Albuquerque went through an urban renewal like many mid-sized cities across America—the old Downtown buildings were torn down to make room for modern office towers surrounded by expanses of concrete. Somehow a small section of tree-lined Gold Street escaped the wrecking ball and Marconi's restaurant survived in the same location. A few other classics remained, such as the Sunshine office building on the next block.

Nancy was drawn to the old architecture on Gold Street, perhaps because of the anthropologist in her who liked to sit and imagine a street one hundred years earlier, as steam locomotives stopped at Alvarado Station, a couple blocks away. She heard rumors Jane led a train tour that left from the station at midnight, which she assumed were idle gossip. She looked at the schedules for the local commuter train, called the Rail Runner, and the Amtrak. No passenger trains departed at midnight from the Alvarado.

She mulled over Marconi's restaurant. If you can call their food Italian, she mused to herself.

Nancy grew up with plenty of traditional Italian cooking, but none of it tasted like Marconi's. The first time she tried their lasagna, she spit it out! It was her first day in Albuquerque, looking at her future quilt shop, after her fainting spell in front of the travel company. Adding to the bizarre day no one warned her what green chile was, or why anyone in their right mind would put such a hot pepper into an otherwise delicious dish of meat, cheese and noodles. As far as she knew, chili was a stew of ground beef and tomato sauce. Fay would later explain Nancy was thinking of what people in New Mexico referred to as Texas chili, a stew of beans, meat and potatoes.

Nancy forever asked Fay about the strange customs of Albuquerque, such as the difference between red and green chile, or why people would want to eat something so hot?

Another issue which irked Nancy was why all the beans? She never acquired a taste for beans or a desire to cook with them. Beans might be okay in a stew, but they lacked absolutely any business near an Italian restaurant, not even in a pasta salad. In her mind, beans were a campfire food, only to be eaten when stranded far from civilization and cooking dinner over a fire from a can.

Nancy wondered about other customs. Why did the young Theresa M call her coffee shop The Jumping Bean Café — after the tourist trinket of Mexican jumping beans — or decorate the café in such a shockingly macabre manner with altars to the dead and skulls everywhere? Nancy heard of Day of the Dead, but she never imagined anyone leaving up Halloween decorations all year long. Why look at death constantly? Wasn't it depressing? Nancy thought the white Calla Lilies were a nice touch, though.

"I suppose," said Nancy, remembering Fay was still in the room, "Marconi's restaurant does okay among businesses on Gold Street. They must have bought the building years ago."

"No. The whole block is owned by old Madame Beesley's son. You don't see much of him. He lets George's real estate office do all the work now, but I hear the old lady used to be very involved with the shops while she was still alive. She walked up and down the street every day, even when she got close to eighty. Mrs. Marconi said she looked at every window display to make sure it changed for every season and wanted everything kept in order. Did you notice how strict the leases are? She made sure her rules were followed. She was the one who stopped the big developers from tearing her buildings down. None of the politicians ever thought about condemning her property. She always got things done the way she wanted them done."

"Too bad she's not around anymore."

Fay gave Nancy a strange look, but decided not to comment.

"Well," continued Nancy, not noticing Fay's expression, "wonder if she could get Marconi's to spiffy up a bit? I don't think their décor has changed in a very long time."

"I told Mrs. Marconi I would be more than happy to help them put together a new look for the restaurant, but it's no use. Mrs. Marconi won't hear of changing anything her late husband decided on. No wonder her daughter wants to sell the place."

Turning abruptly in her seat, Fay admonished Nancy, "You haven't touched your tea! Look, it's gone cold!"

To be polite, Nancy took a swig of the cold liquid. Fay would probably never swill tea in such an improper manner. Nancy looked down at her own clothes. She wore a plain pair of loose fitting pants, nondescript top, and a plain sweater. She couldn't imagine achieving Fay's elegant layered style. Her own attempts at tying a scarf around her neck made Nancy look like a table cloth runner intentionally choked her. She was hopeless in the elegance department.

Today was one of those days when she was going to be inadequate in whatever she thought about. Perhaps getting out of bed was the first bad idea of the day.

Strangely, however, as Fay's tea settled in her stomach, Nancy felt calmness wash over her.

"Have another drink."

Oddly, it sounded like a good idea to Nancy. She tipped back her cup like a drunken sailor and finished the tea.

"Isn't your quilting class going to start soon?"

"Yes," smiled Nancy as a warm buzzy feeling came over her. Suddenly the world didn't seem quite so dark. In fact, now that she thought about some of the issues other business owners on the street dealt with, she didn't feel quite so overwhelmed.

Nancy picked up the stack of bills and stashed them away in her purse. Fay nodded approval.

"My class starts in a couple weeks. I'm getting a better response than I hoped. I put up flyers everywhere I could think of.

I even stuck a flyer in the skull at The Jumping Bean Café. You know the really big skull that you nicknamed Fred the Starving Poet. I think I'll get at least four or five students. Hey, I haven't thought about where I would put a bunch of students in my narrow store. Guess they will work in front with customers."

If Nancy could get the word out about her quilt shop, she might at least start to break even on her expenses. She needed income before she maxed out what little was left of her credit card limits.

"How do you feel?"

Nancy smiled. "Like I suddenly realize everything is going to be okay." Her spirits lifted. "What do you put in this tea anyway?"

As an afterthought she added, "Just joking."

"Oh," said Fay knowingly, "you'll find every business on this block of Gold Street has its own magic."

Nancy was in too sunny of a mood to contemplate Fay's last comment. She happily left the Downtown Tea Shop & Gallery to go next door to Nancy's Quilting. She needed to make arrangements for her future quilting class.

CHAPTER 4

A couple days later Nancy sat in her much too quiet quilt shop when he walked in. She rested comfortably in a patch of warm sunshine which streamed through the front window.

Nancy was certain this gentleman was never in her store before. She found herself catching her breath as she observed him walking slowly down the aisle. Very few men ever wandered into her shop by themselves or accompanied by a female companion. In fact, last week Fay and Nancy installed a bored husband bench in front of their stores to give wives peace to browse tea samples and fabric patterns.

Gay men sometimes frequented Fay's store for unique decorating ideas or special blends of tea. But Nancy's homespun quilt shop, with earthy pattern fabrics and complicated sewing notions, didn't attract men of any stripe.

Nancy suddenly realized opening a quilting store left her almost exclusively in the company of other women. Come to think of it, the rest of the business owners on the street were female. She never considered it before. No wonder she hadn't found a date since moving to Albuquerque. Nor did she acquire any guy pals for skiing or hiking the nearby mountains.

Maybe she was starved for male company. She never considered this aspect of running a quilt store, but it made sense. There weren't any exuberant quilting guys out there. A fellow named Raleigh signed up for her upcoming quilt class, though. Perhaps it was an omen the class would be popular. She crossed her fingers.

Nancy watched the man nervously pace past rows of fabric and distractedly finger sewing supplies. Clearly he was lost, but, like most men, he wouldn't ask for help.

Even if she wasn't male-deprived she would find this man attractive. Nancy felt an instant attraction. She wanted to reach out and trace the stubble across his square chin. She noticed he was trim and square-shouldered, with a hint of hair at the open neckline of his button down shirt. She liked the full head of neatly trimmed gray hair. He was distinguished and dignified while still a bit distressed about visiting a quilt shop. He held up a green checkered pattern fabric next to a contrasting green marble print. What a hideous combination. She figured he wasn't gay.

The gentleman wore business casual clothing, which gave her no clue as to what he did for a living. She was slowly learning that Albuquerque didn't have many rules regarding dress. Fay told her that men came to weddings in a dress shirt and maybe a tie, but no formal dress coat. She even observed funeral attendees in tennis shoes. The banker who stopped in to visit with Fay once in a while wore Dockers and a golf shirt in summer. It was difficult to sort out the highly paid nuclear engineer from the impoverished lifelong graduate student.

Those things never mattered to her. She was lost in the world of academia, with stacks of papers and books. Too many hours of sitting alone in her quilt shop led her to contemplate trivial ideas, such as the identity of the men who walked past her store.

Nancy tried to imagine going on a date with the man. What would be the ideal evening?

They could take the tram to the crest of Sandia Mountains, and watch the city. At the restaurant there they could order romantic drinks as they watched the setting sun snake along the Rio Grande River in shades of yellow and red through the valley floor. Below them they would see city lights appear as twinkling stars across the landscape.

Maybe he was a lawyer and would regal her with tales of drama in the courtroom.

Scratch that. She once dated a lawyer and found him a terrible conversation hog. She didn't need a drama king.

Maybe he was a bohemian musician. Okay, a rather neatly attired one. Perhaps he played chamber music? She could ride with the band in their old van as they crossed the Southwest, and searched for dive bars from the open road. Did classical musicians ever play at roadhouses?

No, on second thought, a working musician might not be a good idea. She dated a Peter Pan-type poet for close to a decade. His philosophy of life, his disdain for the conventional, and his unwillingness to compromise his artistic talent for the conventions of a nine-to-five job seemed intriguing at first. However, his unpredictability when she needed him finally convinced her letting a poet crash on her couch on a regular basis was a bad idea. Even now she was embarrassed to admit how long it took her to tell him to stop coming around.

Her mother always used to say--You can't make a silk purse out of a sow's ear. She'd had similar comments about most of the men Nancy dated. Unfortunately, her mom was right. She vowed she would do better in Albuquerque.

Nancy turned her attention back to her work. She almost worked up the courage to talk with the unfamiliar man in her store when the front door opened, and another man walked in, leading an older woman by the hand, presumably his mother. She carried a bright floral shawl over her arm.

They looked to be Indian. No, she corrected herself; shouldn't she refer to them as Native Americans? She guessed the son was in his forties and the mother closer to her in age. Would this be Nancy, walking into a store with her grown child, if she chose to have kids? It was a strange thing to contemplate.

The mother and son walked directly over to her, but when they stopped to speak, Nancy noticed they didn't look her directly in the eyes. Instead, the mother lifted her shawl for Nancy to examine.

"Hello," said the woman while staring out of Nancy's window instead of looking at her. Her son stood respectfully off to the side. Nancy couldn't recall if she ever noticed two men in her store at the same time since opening to the public.

"Can you make another shawl like this one?" inquired the woman.

Nancy turned her attention to the fabric at hand. She noticed an unfortunate rip near the edge, which explained the need for a replacement. Too bad. The shawl was a cheerful bright yellow with a blue floral pattern and long fringe around the edges.

"You must have owned this a long time."

Fabric goes through fads, just like car colors or household paint. Once the manufacturer uses up a dye lot in a season, a new color palette replaces it for the next round of production. Over time, it becomes nearly impossible to match color patterns. A pattern fabric from the 60s looks different from floral pattern from the 40s, not to mention the fiber content goes in cycles as well.

Nancy turned the fabric over in her hands, but she was stumped. She couldn't place it. The weight and weave of the cloth felt rather modern, but not overly synthetic, like she would expect of the 1970s, yet the vibrant colors screamed 1978.

She started to explain, "I, umm, don't actually sew anything, umm, here in the store."

"You don't sew?" asked the surprised woman. "I thought it said 'Nancy's Quilting' on the sign."

"Umm, yeah, I mean no," Nancy stammered. "I mean to say I only sell quilting supplies. I do sew, but not usually in the store. Well, just when I bring a project from home or I teach a class." Nancy found herself talking in circles. Why did she feel unprepared to deal with customers?

She contemplated the fabric further. "I don't even know where you could find fabric like this. Is this an heirloom?"

The mother and son glanced at each other, trying to decide how much they should explain about their culture. Nancy waited patiently.

"Well," said the mother, "I use this shawl for my dances out at Zuni Pueblo. I need to replace it in time for next weekend. It's not old. But, as you can see, it unfortunately got damaged."

"Not old. That's interesting. It's been a long time since I noticed any fabric bolts with these particular colors, many years ago."

Nancy wondered if the shawls were made in a sacred manner. Did they practice a special ritual to honor Native American traditions? Did the medicine men of the village decide what color the women could use, the way elder men of an Amish community decided what colors and patterns the women could use in an Amish quilt?

Later a friend would explain the Zunis were matriarchal. While the mother was reticent to talk about her culture, she didn't answer to elder men.

"Usually," said the woman, as if reading Nancy's mind, "I order a new shawl when I need it, but they are expensive and take a while to ship. I don't have time to wait. Besides, I thought your store might be cheaper."

This was not the answer Nancy was hoped for. She didn't want to compete in bargain shopping. She sighed, but decided to make the best of it.

"Where do you find these colors?"

"We have a factory in Sweden print the cloth and sew the shawls special for us," said the woman brightly.

"Oh," was all Nancy answered.

Nancy contemplated the situation further. She decided she wanted to help. She offered to make a shawl using the quilting technique of appliquéing floral print cut-out flowers on a yellow background, but that would take time. The woman seemed to understand and said that some of the other dancers used similar shawls. In the end they decided Nancy could patch the damaged shawl for the woman to use until a new one arrived from Sweden.

The son spoke up for the first time and offered to pick up the shawl when the repair was complete. He explained he was a lawyer, and worked the next block over in the Sunshine office building. Nancy chatted with mother and son, reassured she did have the ability to run her quilt store.

It was only after the mother and son left Nancy realized two things. One, she wasn't sure she should get into the business of sewing for other people, even if it was a repair. Tailoring was never part of her business plan. But she became so caught up in the moment of helping a customer she didn't stop to think about whether she should take on the project or not. Okay, one time wouldn't hurt. She wasn't busy doing anything else. However, she recalled reading about the need for a business to stay focused. She would spend more time figuring out what she should and shouldn't do in the future.

Didn't one of her friends back home remind her she hadn't set up a website yet? Nancy made a note to get started. She would have to find the money somewhere. After being an employee for so many years she didn't think of everything she should do. Her life used to run on an academic cycle of semesters. In Albuquerque she was left to chart her own course. She read about how more and more retail business is done online and all the different types of social media used by businesses. It got confusing and overwhelming sometimes.

However, Nancy's other realization bothered her more. The attractive, yet mysterious, fellow who looked at green fabrics slipped out of her shop while she helped with the shawl. She didn't even get the chance to see the color of his eyes.

CHAPTER 5

Nancy and Fay settled into a table by the front window of the Standard Diner. The restaurant was built from an old gas station. Or was it a car dealership? Nancy couldn't remember now. Everyone in her neighborhood insisted she try the food.

Nancy admired the chic updates to the sleek 1930s Streamline Moderne architecture. It was similar to buildings found in cities like Miami, but with a Southwest touch. She remarked upon it to Fay, adding that she liked the interior with its contemporary Art Deco, exposed brick and ductwork, and accented with pink ceiling lighting. The booths and chairs were padded in chocolate brown leather, hinting at a classic diner.

"Shall we share some wine?" asked Fay.

"Ah, there's nothing like a Sunday evening." Nancy perused the wine list at a leisurely pace. Both the Downtown Tea Shop & Gallery and Nancy's Quilting were closed on Mondays, so Sunday was their equivalent of a Friday night out.

"Plans for tomorrow?"

"The usual," said Nancy. "I'm going to work on my house."

Nancy lived in the historic Huning Highland neighborhood, near the restaurant. Standard Diner sat on Central Avenue, which used to be the legendary Route 66. In the 1950s, the interstate freeway system was built, and Route 66 all but abandoned. The old stores were boarded up as people flocked to the new mall in the suburbs. People avoided going downtown if they could help it because the area became shabby.

"Would you believe," asked Fay thinking similar thoughts, "this neighborhood still used to have its share of druggies and hookers when I moved to town?"

The neighborhood was later christened "EDo" for East Downtown. The rebranding effort worked. It was becoming hip and trendy.

"I hear my neighbors talk about how bad it used to be."

Fay pursed her lips. "Not just the houses. See the lofts across the street? Used to be the old Albuquerque high school. It sat boarded up with an ugly chain link fence for many years. It used to drag the entire neighborhood down. And see the old drive-thru hot dog stand up the street? It used to be called Pop-n-Taco. Always had prostitutes hanging around it. Day and night."

Nancy's neighborhood was still not fully gentrified by any stretch of the imagination, but she constantly heard stories about how bad it used to be.

She debated buying a house as a single woman in an area still rough around the edges, but it reminded her of home. She craved tree-lined streets with dusty Victorian houses. She never tired of creaking sash windows, sagging floors, and numerous handmade details that made each residence unique. She didn't know how anyone could live in a cookie cutter subdivision where every stucco house displayed a garage door in front. How did they find the right one at night? They all looked almost exactly the same.

In addition to opening her store, Nancy took on the project of dealing with an old dwelling with fixtures and pipes that always needed fixed in house more than a hundred years old. Of course it was a challenge when she also lacked money. The conversation reminded Nancy she still hadn't figured out where to find the mortgage payment by the end of the month. She wondered how long it would take for the wine to arrive.

"I never would consider buying a home in this area when I moved to town more than a decade ago," said Fay. She owned a sensible single story ranch house in the Country Club neighborhood. Fay's part of town was always high class, or so Nancy was told.

Nancy liked the majestic old trees and big green lawns in Fay's neighborhood, a rare treat in the desert southwest. But the sad little cottage she found at the edge of Country Club while house hunting was out of her comfortable price range.

Nancy glanced back out the window. "Doesn't Rachel live near here?"

"I believe she lives right across the street."

Nancy never saw Rachel at any of the neighborhood meetings, but given how many hours the young woman worked, it didn't surprise her.

"Do you ever wish you bought a condo instead of a house?" asked Nancy. Maybe life would be easier if she owned a small place requiring little care.

"No. Look at all those young people coming in and out of the building across the street. Would you really want to hear their music, or put up with them coming and going in the middle of the night?"

Nancy never considered that angle before.

"My friend Bunny," said Fay, "moved to Florida after her beloved Hank died. Thought she would enjoy a new life with fun and sun in Miami. She paid good money for one of those ritzy new condos in a glass high rise on the ocean with the most beautiful views from the balcony." Leaning forward Fay continued, "And do you know what happened?"

"No," replied Nancy reflexively.

"The real estate market went bust, that's what happened." Fay gathered steam. "Oh, dear. What a nightmare for poor Bunny. At first they told her the HOA dues would go through the roof because only a few condos sold in the building, so the few owners would need to make up for the entire building. Well, they got a lawyer and made sure the developer couldn't stick them with extra costs, but it only got worse."

"How?"

"The developer," said Fay, lowering her voice, "decided to solve his financial problems by converting the rest of the unsold units into rentals. All of a sudden, Bunny lives with a bunch of rowdy kids running around the halls."

"Families?"

"No. Kids in college. Up all night, drinking and carrying on. You would think those young people do something, like study, or get a job, but apparently not. No respect whatsoever."

Fay shook her head in a tsk-tsk manner. She sat up straighter and continued her story.

"Well, Bunny was beside herself. This was not how she planned to spend her golden years. Trash in the hallways. Loud music at the BBQ. One day she found the entire swimming pool full of plastic pink flamingos. That was the last straw."

Nancy tried not to laugh at the thought of dozens of pink flamingos bobbing in a pool.

Fay sat back in her chair and continued, "Of course, Bunny couldn't sell because the real estate market crashed. She and the other condo owners were stuck."

Nancy mumbled a polite, "How awful."

"Hmm," said Fay in agreement. "Well, Bunny eventually rounded up the other condo owners and set a strict set of rules for those awful renters. Turns out the renters don't get any votes for the condo by-laws. There weren't supposed to be renters in the first place. But the bank already took over the bankrupt building from the developer by the time they realized they could vote new by-laws. And the bank didn't really care what the owners did. The bank never watches the building very closely."

Fay gave a triumphant smile.

Nancy was trying to imagine a gray haired lady named Bunny.

Fay sat upright. "Those condo owners ensure everything gets done right. They created special committees to look after everything in the building. The kids can't run around trashing everything. They must pay fines or lose their security deposits for issues like music too loud at night."

"Can they do that?"

"I don't know," answered Fay, "but they have. No more monkey business. The place is slowly turning back into the sophisticated complex Bunny wanted."

Nancy decided that she had made a good choice to open her store instead of heading to an old folk's community in Florida. She had heard stories of elderly vigilante groups roaming their neighborhoods looking for violations, such as leaving a trash can in the driveway. Punishment was swift and harsh.

"Sometimes I think about joining Bunny," said Fay quietly.

Nancy's head jerked up in surprise. "You can't be serious!"

"Well, why are we here? We don't have decent shopping. I think Nordstrom will open in Antarctica before they come to Albuquerque. I often hear the city is going to grow; wait until we get to one million people and everything will be different, but I don't know. Bunny tells me my store would do a hundred times better in Miami. People spend a lot more money on decorating or enjoying fine tea in a bigger city."

"Bunny just wants you to buy a condo in her building," sulked Nancy.

Nancy never knew Fay to talk about leaving Gold Street. How sad would that be for the quilt shop? What if Fay's space was filled with some horrible store? What if Nancy ended up next to a tattoo parlor? They seemed popular in Albuquerque.

"You can't leave. You're my first official friend here."

"Well dear, I need to consider all of my options. Bunny said some of the old gals are thinking about leaving the Boston area and going to Miami. I may be the first of our gang to lose my husband, but some of the other old gals are now on their own as well. What fun it would be to have all my best girlfriends back together in one place. Just like old times. What a hoot."

"But you can't leave!" exclaimed Nancy, more passionately than she expected.

Fay gave her a smile.

"Don't you know of any reasons to stay?"

Fay seemed to murmur an answer, but not loud enough for Nancy to hear. It was like she couldn't quite bring herself to tell Nancy what it was.

Nancy looked at Fay expectantly. Fay seemed to mull over sharing a confidence, but instead, she abruptly pulled out a menu and began to remark on the food.

"Oh look. They have Onion Fried Calamari. And here is Watermelon and Tuna Ceviche."

Nancy peered more closely at the Ceviche appetizer on the menu. "They put green chile on Sashimi tuna?" She was disgusted. "That is wrong. The whole green chile thing in New Mexico is out of control."

However, some of the menu items stirred a deep longing in Nancy's soul. She craved Midwestern style comfort food. Here was a restaurant with some of her favorites, but in a more contemporary style.

Her mouth watered at the thought of cinnamon baked brie made with an apple compote and port wine reduction. She could smell warm apple aroma when it was served at a nearby table. She jealously watched as the diners stroked melting brie cheese across their piping hot fresh bread.

Brie didn't count as traditional food in her home state of Indiana, although you could make an argument for apples, with the Johnny Appleseed thing, and they were definitely big into cheeses.

She lost herself in thinking about the entrees: bacon wrapped meatloaf covered in red wine gravy, a Philly cheese steak sandwich made from slow roasted prime rib with Gruyere cheese, or a chicken fried steak with peppercorn cream gravy.

But when their orders were taken, the macaroni and cheese, made with Guinness and an Irish cheddar sauce, was irresistible to Nancy.

Nancy pictured her grandmother at the old family farmhouse. Ma started her day with black coffee and a cigarette, then the shrunken, but nimble, old woman would busy herself with all types of quilting, crocheting and baking. She was Nancy's favorite relative to visit while growing up.

Her absolute favorite memory of her grandmother was when Ma made macaroni and cheese from scratch. Nancy never saw her use a box mix. Instead, her grandmother melted real butter mixed with farm heavy cream, then added a dash of corn starch to thicken the sauce, and then slowly stirred in chunks of hard Swiss cheese. It was glorious to eat--not like powered cheese stuff.

Nancy was so lost in thought about her grandmother she almost didn't see him.

It was the distinguished man from her shop. He walked by the front window of the diner, chatting on his cell phone. Fay observed Nancy looking out the window and peered more closely herself.

"Good heavens," said Fay. "I believe I know that gentleman. I'm sure I must."

"Really? He came into my store the other day."

"Whatever on earth for?"

Nancy scowled, but answered truthfully, "I don't know. Other customers walked in, I got busy, and he left before I had a chance to find out." Nancy added hopefully, "Do you know him?"

"He's quite a looker."

"Do you know him?" repeated Nancy. She noticed a certain look in Fay's eyes. The kind of look a woman has only when a man catches her attention. Maybe she should back down.

"So he's a friend of yours?" tried Nancy again, as respectfully as she could ask.

"No. I am trying to figure out how I know him. Was he that special friend of Stella the evil witch?" She gave a shudder.

Clearly Fay found the idea distasteful.

Fay looked relieved. "No, that can't be it. Stella's friend was rather bald. But I think maybe he is a friend of a friend somehow. I'm sure I heard his voice. It's somehow deep and calming. Now why would I remember that about him?"

Nancy and Fay contemplated the man further. "Perhaps he came into the tea shop?" inquired Nancy.

"No, he has not. I'm sure of it."

Nancy breathed a sigh of relief.

Fay shot her a dirty look.

"Well Fay, you know mostly gay men seek out your shop."

Fay conceded the point.

The two women watched as the mystery man passed up the street. Was he treating a woman to a fabulous dinner at the Artichoke Café up the block? Nancy was tempted to try the restaurant, except it was clearly out of her current budget. Maybe Mystery Man was meeting his wife of twenty years to celebrate their anniversary at the pizza parlor. Why did she even care?

Nancy paused to think about wedding anniversaries. All at once it hit her. Of course, no wonder she was a little off her rocker. Every year it caught her by surprise. It was her and Bobby's wedding anniversary. If they stayed married, that is. Maybe the date still bothered her because she never replaced it with a new anniversary. She needed a happy new one to stop thinking about the old one every year.

Nancy and Bobby would have passed their fortieth wedding anniversary a couple years ago. How strange was that to think about? Bobby long since remarried, so maybe he would eventually make a big four-oh celebration.

Nancy tried to forget the email she recently received from her former brother-in-law. Will was a congenial fellow, and she always got on well with him. They stayed in touch over the years, but this wasn't one of Will's usual forwarded emails of jokes or politics. Bobby's cancer returned.

She allowed herself one indulgent thought, and then she would completely shut it out of her mind. What if she and Bobby currently celebrated their forty-second wedding anniversary at some little university café in Indiana, surrounded by a lifetime of friends? Would it prevent his cancer from coming back? Had the young drama queen he married sucked the life out of him?

She knew she was acting petty. It was hard to imagine who Nancy would be if she stayed married these past forty-some years.

She knew she wouldn't start a new chapter of her life sitting in a diner in Albuquerque. It was hard enough to convince Bobby to try new vacation spots. He never wanted to leave the place where he grew up. It looked like he would get his wish.

She, on the other hand, felt like she started a new beginning, a second chance to do things right this time. When their wine arrived, Nancy proposed a toast, "Here is to fresh new beginnings."

The food in front of them smelled absolutely delicious.

Nancy closed her eyes as she brought the wonderfully creamy mac-n-cheese to her lips.

"Jesus and mother of Mary!" exclaimed Nancy, loudly enough for the other diners to notice, as she spit the mouthful of food into her napkin.

Fay looked worried. "Dear, whatever is wrong?"

Tears came to Nancy's eyes as she explained. "They put green chile in my macaroni and cheese!"

CHAPTER 6

Fay and Nancy made a quick mid-morning stop at the Jumping Bean Café before opening their stores, when Theresa M pulled out a copy of the Alibi, a weekly local alternative newspaper.

"This ad must be you Nancy," said Theresa M.

"Whatever are you talking about?" asked Fay.

The three women sat down together at one of the small tables. They barely managed to squeeze around it. Theresa M flipped to the back of the paper, a section Fay and Nancy never read.

"Look," pointed out Theresa M. She circled the tiny print in the "I Saw You" category of the personals. They read the ad together.

GOLD STREET
ME: Looking for a quilter.
YOU: The new girl in town.
WE: Could climb under a blanket together.

"Climb under a blanket together? What kind of introduction is that?" asked Nancy.

Fay wrinkled her nose. "Really."

"But all the ads sound that way," said Theresa M. They read more and Theresa M was right. If anything, the Gold Street ad was one of the tamest.

"That's you," said Theresa M again to Nancy. "Aren't you going to answer the ad to find out who it was? I would. Otherwise I would look at every guy walking down the street and wonder if he was the one."

Theresa M had a point.

Better a stalker is known than unknown.

Theresa M said, "I read the ads every week to see what guys might be checking me and my friends out." Almost under her breath she added, "Who knew it works for old ladies, too?"

Fay and Nancy decided to ignore Theresa M's last comment. After much discussion, they decided Nancy should reply to the ad. Theresa M gave her the instructions about how to proceed, and, like a mother hen, she insisted Nancy pick a very public restaurant, tell everyone where she went, and text updates throughout the meal.

Fay gave a stern look. "Young lady, it is quite rude to text other people while sitting with a date at a nice dinner. Is that how you treat the young men who ask you out for a special evening?"

Theresa M couldn't help rolling her eyes. "Mostly I just hook up," She didn't explain any further.

Nancy decided it was just as well Fay didn't know what Theresa M meant by the term hooking up-- Theresa M didn't go on sweet dates with young bobby socks boys who arrived in their dads' borrowed cars to go to a malt shop or drive in. Dating changed quite a bit since Fay was young. Being a college professor, Nancy spent her career around the changing landscape of young love. Kids went out in groups, everyone paying dutch. Afterwards, a couple "hooked up" for a short time, perhaps only the night. Young women now buy themselves a house instead of worry about finding a man to put a ring on their finger. Nancy was divorced before she ever considered making a major purchase by herself. Then again, women weren't legally entitled to sign their own mortgages until the mid-seventies, around the time of her divorce. There was no way she could buy a house by herself fresh out of college.

Nancy looked at the other two women. Fay continued to lecture Theresa M on proper conduct for dates with young men. Nancy did a quick calculation in her head and figured Fay started dating in the early 1950s. She could picture the older woman in a corset, twin sweater set and a single strand of pearls.

However, it occurred to Nancy she was as unskilled at navigating modern love as Fay. She constantly read disturbing magazine articles, such as one about how older women were following the kids in sexting—sending text messages with naked pictures of themselves to men they dated, and various other dating habits Nancy felt fully unprepared to embrace.

"Do you really think a blind date is a good idea?" asked Nancy, interrupting Fay's lecture on proper behavior.

"Yes," they both replied emphatically.

Nancy continued to mull it over. Fay was probably hoping Nancy would develop a new love interest and stop talking about the Mystery Man she and Fay observed from the window of the Standard Diner the other night. He was the one who looked at green fabric in her store.

Wait a minute, thought Nancy to herself. Could it be the Mystery Man who placed the ad in the paper? He was too shy to talk with Nancy in her shop, or so she liked to think. Picturing him arriving on a blind date was a glorious thought, and so was the possibility of another man as dignified and potentially interesting as the Mystery Man.

Up until that point, Nancy wasn't sure she would actually follow through with the ad. But who could resist the idea of spending the evening with the Mystery Man? And bragging about it to Fay the next day? Not that she was competitive or anything. She smiled to herself. It was a long time since she went on a proper date.

Nancy thought about more romantic date ideas. Her Mystery Man could turn out to be athletic. They could ski nearby or rent snow shoes. Despite it being rather warm and mild in the city during most of winter, the mountains were packed with snow. Except when she thought about it, she wasn't sure she could still stand up on a pair of skis. She spent a lot of time lately sitting in her store.

She and her date could take the Rail Runner train to Santa Fe for the day. Winter dumped plenty of snow on the ground in the City Different. They could wander the winding streets until they found a quaint adobe restaurant to warm themselves next to a roaring flame in a Kiva fireplace. Or they could venture to seemingly endless galleries along Canyon Road, discussing the finer points of art. She would discover he harbored a quirky interest in Russian painters of the nineteenth century.

Scratch that. One of her friends from home phoned the other day to describe a horrible date which wouldn't end. Seems a day at the rodeo isn't much fun if your blind date is psycho. Perhaps she should think about some shorter date options.

What if her date dazzled her with his knowledge of unique restaurants around Albuquerque? He would tell her he found a surprise to show her in Old Town. They would meet and browse through the sculpture garden in front of the art and history museum. He would lead her along the stone paths until they reached a wild area with a marker. He would explain they were going to Numbe Whageh—a Native American name for Our Center Place. He would read aloud, "From the beginning of time, life has swirled within and around Numbe Whageh, our Pueblo center place." After finishing the poem he would show her a hidden pathway going down into the middle of a secret garden, and stop to sit for a few minutes on the stones. They would admire the clear blue sky with a few puffy clouds on the horizon.

Next he would lead her through a maze of streets and plazas in Old Town until they arrived at another hidden surprise at the back of a courtyard—the Capilla de Nuestra Senora de Guadalupe. He would tell her the strange history of the nun who built the little adobe chapel in honor of Our Lady of Guadalupe. It remained open night and day for the faithful to light candles and leaves messages for their dearly departed at the altars. She would look through the hand-written notes, pictures and mementos left in honor of the beloved amid the candles.

He would read to her one of the inscriptions carved into the panels on the walls, "My Soul Hath Desired Thee In The Night, And With My Spirit Within Me, In The Morn Early, I Will Watch To Thee."

She would notice the odd big round plastic window at the north end of the chapel and wonder about the green color crossed with a white grid, surrounded by a ring of blue at the outer edge patterned with red circles. She couldn't recall seeing a window like it before. He would explain it was actually a perpetual calendar made from three sheets of plexiglass, which someone rotated at the beginning of the year to show Our Lady of Guadalupe Feast Days by the moon phases. She liked to think the center sphere represented the sun. She would remember the long ago John Denver song as she touched it, and the crazy dream would come true.

Later, as if the evening couldn't get any better, he would lead her to the back of a tucked away plaza to a cozy French restaurant. They would sit at one of only four tables in the room, eating the most magnificent crepes. They would celebrate finding each other over a bottle of champagne, toasting their lucky fortune well into the night.

"What are you going to wear?" Nancy vaguely heard someone ask. She looked up and realized Fay and Theresa M were watching her expectantly.

What am I going to wear? Nancy asked herself. Do I even know how to dress up for a date anymore?

****

A couple of evenings later, after answering the ad, Nancy found herself at a chain restaurant at Cottonwood Mall. She watched a perky young waitress in black t-shirt haul mounds of food across the room. She shifted uncomfortably in the plastic booth as she studied the specials. This month the triple-decker gourmet cheeseburger could be accompanied by a "Winter Ski Trip" milkshake—Coors beer and Rocky Mountain Peach Whiskey, mixed with Mountain Dew ice cream. She noted the option of beer cheese or beer mustard for dipping the fries. Involuntarily she gave a shudder. She never acquired a taste for beer.

Giant flat screen T.V.s surrounded the walls, and each one broadcasted a different sports game. She glanced from a football game, to a sports analysis, to basketball. None held her attention.

Nancy became so busy since arriving in Albuquerque she never got around to exploring the west part of town, across the river. The Westside neighborhoods sprung up new developments like jackrabbits hopping out of the mesa. Most of the subdivisions of endless houses were built in the last twenty or thirty years.

Nancy felt rather lost. She never felt the desire to buy a newer home. She was, after all, a traditional quilter. She was the kind of gal who thrived in historic buildings. She tried looking up a bookstore on the Westside. She figured she could spend some time browsing while she was in the area, but she didn't find anything beyond Hastings and book departments at Target and Wal-Mart. That couldn't be right, could it? Surely there was a small book seller or dusty used book shop.

Okay, the whole blind date thing on the Westside wasn't starting off right. She would feel better once her date actually arrived. The fellow might work close by, although Nancy didn't see many office buildings. Her Mystery Man could live in an apartment building. There were some nice complexes. He could be helping an elderly mother nearby or something...

Nancy nervously twiddled the paper from her straw. She kept her eyes glued on the door as she continued to make guesses about her blind date. She arrived early to stake out a table. Her blind date was supposed to arrive carrying a single red rose, which sounded romantic when they traded emails earlier in the week, although now it seemed awkward. Nancy began to doubt herself. Why was a woman in her sixties acting like a school girl?

Nancy definitely started to lose her nerve. She contemplated bolting out the door when she caught sight of a man coming through the door with a limp red flower in his hands.

Nancy's heart quickened. Would she finally meet the Mystery Man who came into her store? Obviously this man was not him, unless there was some horrible mistake. Could two men arrive at the restaurant at 7 PM, both carrying red roses? Nancy knew that wasn't likely. Her heart sank as he approached the table. He, of course, knew her from the quilt shop. He could identify her, but she wouldn't recognize him.

Or did she?

As he drew close to the table, Nancy realized she knew the younger, yet balding, man with a moustache and paunch belly. He was from Marconi's restaurant. It was Mary Ann's husband carrying the wilting rose!

With a deep sinking feeling as he approached the table, Nancy knew it was Carmen's son-in-law. Carmen never found good things to say about him. Mary Ann generally didn't look happy either, although Nancy assumed she was worn out from running the restaurant while raising kids and taking care of her aging mother.

The husband walked up to her with a sickly smile. No wonder he asked to meet her on the Westside, away from their restaurant and everyone who knew them Downtown, and away from his family in the Northeast Heights.

For once, Nancy's mind went blank. She couldn't find words to say to him. She dashed out the door, barely remembering her coat. It was only as she started her car she remembered to text Theresa M: Men suck. Dating bad idea.

When Fay later asked about Nancy's evening, all Nancy would answer is the blind date was totally unappealing and she was done with strange men. Technically speaking, her blind date wasn't a complete stranger, since she saw Mary Ann's husband in passing several times. But she let that one go. After all, the guy did count as strange.

Nancy wasn't sure why she didn't confide in Fay or get her advice about handling the situation.

Certainly Nancy wasn't going to say anything to Mary Ann. It just wasn't her place. The whole situation was a disaster. Maybe she didn't want to make Fay an accomplice to the whole sordid affair. Although, upon further reflection, Nancy admitted to herself she wasn't noble. She didn't know what to say.

Nancy was sure of one thing. She was finished with Mystery Men.

When Theresa M later told Nancy she saw Mary Ann smiling, carrying a dozen red roses from her husband (or was it eleven?), Nancy was ready to crawl in a hole and stay away from love forever.

CHAPTER 7

Nancy pulled a long table away from the wall and set up a group of chairs in her store. As the cold January evening approached, she was finally ready for her first quilting class to meet.

In the days since The Blind Date from Hell, Nancy totally applied herself to working with a web developer to get her website ready and live. Now, instead of spending her days in boredom between customers, she updated website content, posted new items, found links, and worked on her first electronic newsletter.

She joined Facebook years back to stay in touch with her students at the college. She found they communicated more readily online than dropping by during her office hours. While setting up her store she was faced with a decision. Should she set up a new Facebook page to represent her business, or continue to communicate with the hundreds she already added to on her personal page? In the end, she decided she was her business. She never talked about anything else anyway, so she started posting to her existing Facebook page about her new quilt shop website.

The strategy worked. Friends and former students seemed to enjoy her posts about the store. She got good traffic on her new website. Although there still weren't a lot of people walking through her door, people around the country browsed her merchandise online.

Nancy knew she needed to figure out how to take her business to the next level. She traded emails with some successful small craft stores around the country. Most of them told her the same thing--she needed to find some kind of specialized niche to get customers from around the country to buy from her, instead of their local stores, particularly the big chains which sold at deep volume discounts. She could never compete successfully with Wal-Mart.

For tonight, though, Nancy's sole focus was getting through her first quilt class. Eight people enrolled. She was overjoyed. She would have felt successful if she enrolled half that number of students.

Nancy set out coffee and snacks as the first people arrived. Once almost everyone was settled, she made her introductions. "Hello everyone and welcome to my quilt sampler class. Are you familiar with traditional stitch samplers? We're going to learn how to make something similar. Small mini-quilts to finish during our six weeks together. Our tiny completed quilts will be about the size of a piece of notebook paper."

"For the design, we're going to work with recycled household fabric scraps. If you don't have anything around your house, I have a bucket of fabric pieces by the front door."

As she spoke, the last couple of students made their way to the table. Nancy talked about the tradition of recycling old linens and clothes into quilts. How it was very environmentally friendly and earlier generations couldn't afford to throw fabric away, even the smallest scraps. Everything needed to be reused. She also gave a short lecture on classic quilt patterns in the United States and passed around coffee table books for inspiration. In particular she talked about symbols used in Midwestern quilt patterns.

Nancy turned to her students to make introductions.

A neatly dressed woman in a business suit and glasses started. Nancy guessed she was in her fifties.

"Hi, I'm Ann. I recently opened my own CPA firm in the Sunshine building. I used to work at Sandia Labs, but I decided it was time to open my own office Downtown. I'm married and have three kids." She added, "I joined the class because I'm looking for some sort of craft project to slow down and reduce my stress level. I saw the class flyer hanging in the lobby of the Sunshine building and thought it sounded like fun."

"Quilting can be very relaxing," Nancy interjected.

"I hope so," replied Ann. "Plus, I wanted to spend time with my friend Janice." Ann turned and smiled at the woman seated next to her.

Nancy would guess Janice was about the same age as her friend Ann, but she sported longer hair and more casual clothes.

"Hi," said Janice softly. "I live next door to Ann, by the foothills on the far east side of town. Since Ann opened her business here, she keeps telling me I should try doing something Downtown. Guess I don't really get down here much. I just never think of it."

"Tell us something about yourself," Nancy prodded.

"Oh, not much to tell," said Janice. "Let's see. I have two kids close in age to Ann's. My husband is stationed at Kirtland Air Force Base and about ready to retire. So I never really worked. We're thinking about where to retire."

"Taking care of a family is work," said one of the women.

"Amen," added another.

Nancy looked around in relief. Her class seemed to cover all the generations and even included a man. She worried about whether they would get along.

"Oh," added Janice, "I used to sew a lot. But usually with a sewing machine and from store bought patterns. Taking a class to design my own project and hand sew it seemed like a big challenge. I hope I'm up to it, because I'm actually pretty nervous."

Ann gave her friend Janice a reassuring smile.

Nancy began to get the uncomfortable feeling something more must be going on with Janice. She didn't seem to feel any confidence in herself.

The next woman at the table flaunted beautiful long hair most of the way down her back. Nancy guessed she was in her early thirties. "I'm Trish," she said. "I'm a teacher living on the Westside with my little guy Nathan. He's a really great kid. But, umm, I just got divorced and was looking for something to do while my son is with his dad or my parents. I wanted to get out of the house. I'm totally not ready for the bar scene or anything like that. I just wanted to hang out with new people and try new things. Quilting sounded like fun. Oh, I saw your flyer when my friend and I ate lunch the other day at Marconi's."

Stay away from Marconi's, Nancy thought.

The next student looked even younger than Trish. Nancy assumed she couldn't be twenty-five. She was fashionably dressed and naturally radiated energy and beauty.

"Hey, I'm Keisha," said the stylish gal. "I just finished college at UNM, so I now work at the mall."

A couple other students groaned. It must be hard to finish school in such a difficult economy. Plenty of people told Nancy she was crazy to start a business while retail did so badly. Then again, Nancy knew there were folks who discouraged trying anything new. She also understood she seized a window of opportunity with little competition. Few new stores entered the market. If only she could establish a stronghold in a niche.

"So anyway," continued Keisha, "I'm trying out different things to see what I might be interested in doing. Like, since I can't get a real job, why not find something really cool?"

"You want to make quilt samplers?" asked one of the other students.

"I don't know about quilting. Maybe," answered Keisha. "My friend Theresa M owns the Jumping Bean Café across the street. That's where I saw your flyer. Anyway, we know people who farm here and in the South Valley. People who make things to sell from what they produce. I thought it would be cool to check it out."

Keisha added, "We know lots of girls who knit and make their own yarn. That's kind of a big thing already. But we can't think of anyone who quilts or even hand sews. I think I want to find something I can make with my hands."

"There are farms here?" asked Nancy in wonder.

"Yes," replied several students at the same time.

Keisha explained, "Even though this is Downtown, it's still the valley. Well, technically, Central Avenue splits the North Valley from the South Valley. The quilt shop is part of the South Valley because we are a block south. People farmed in the valley along the river for a very long time. Places like Old Town and Barelas are really old farming villages settled by the Spanish."

"The divide is why people fought over the name Albuquerque," remarked another person.

Nancy looked puzzled.

Keisha patiently explained further. "Right now we're by the train station. When the train came through in the late 1800's, they wanted to name the new railroad town Albuquerque, but the Hispanic village and fort by the river, a couple miles away, already was Albuquerque. So the older village became Old Town and this was New Town. Both became Albuquerque in the end."

Someone else added, "The two Albuquerques didn't merge for a long time."

Nancy reflected the history explained a lot. Albuquerque was a crossroads of different cultures, but they often don't quite mesh together. Nancy wondered which Native Americans lived in the valley before either the Spanish fort was settled or the train came through. The old Spanish Camino Real was traveled by Spanish traders for hundreds of years up the river valley, but the indigenous Turquoise trade routes from Central America were probably a thousand or more years old.

Another woman spoke up. "Thinking about farming—you'll have to check out the Growers Market at Robinson Park in the summer. They have the usual stuff, like vegetables. But people stand in line for the almond chocolate croissants freshly baked from the French bakery. And special items like local honey. A lot of urban bee keepers live here."

Keisha said, "Best of all is in the fall they roast huge bags of green chile. It smells great!"

"I can hardly wait," replied Nancy, a little too sarcastically. She couldn't imagine why anyone would need an enormous amount of green chile, roasted or not.

Next at the table was a dapper man Nancy guessed to be close to her own age.

"Hello, everyone!" he said enthusiastically. "I'm Raleigh. I'm originally from Georgia, but lived in Old Town for the last forty years. Which practically makes me a New Mexico native." He smiled at everyone.

Raleigh went on to explain, "I saw the flyer next door at the fabulous tea shop and gallery. Fay, the proprietor, is such a doll. I always find something special in her emporium."

The last statement answered one of Nancy's questions about Raleigh, although Nancy couldn't imagine being attracted to him anyway. With freshly ironed clothes and a scarf tied neatly around his neck, he was what is referred to in certain circles as a Nelly—a rather feminine gay man.

"I am so excited to be here with all of you wonderful and talented ladies," said Raleigh with natural southern charm. "I wasn't sure about taking the class. I'm nervous like Janice. I'm an artist and always look for new ways to express myself. And, as the lovely Keisha pointed out, quilting is going to be the 'new' knitting, I'm sure of it. I figured hey, even if I can't sew, which I don't, I always enjoy making collages out of different types of materials. There must be some way for me to work in fabric. I mean," said Raleigh pausing a moment for drama, "don't they make those little sticky strips you use to iron pieces of fabric together? I've seen them used for stage costumes."

"You don't sew?" clarified Nancy.

"Oh, my heavens, no," replied Raleigh, fanning himself. "And no interest in learning. Darling, my big clumsy man fingers don't grab and pump things quite that small."

Raleigh let the double meaning of his words drift through the group for a few moments. Nancy was a loss for words when the woman to Raleigh's left spoke up.

"Perhaps we could find you something bigger to hold," snickered a younger punkish woman who appeared to Nancy to be in her late twenties. Nancy looked again and decided punk wasn't quite the right description. However, she definitely wore her own style, wearing dark glasses even though it was already evening, big hoop earrings, hair that frizzled almost into an afro, and an Asian-style chocker collar necklace with large red beads and shells hanging down.

The young woman explained, "I'm Aen. Spelled A-E-N, but pronounced as 'Ann' like the other Ann who's in the class tonight."

Nancy supposed it might get confusing with two "Anns" in the class, although it would be impossible to mistake one for the other. They appeared to be polar opposites in personality.

Aen continued, "So I'm, like, a musician and performance artist. Like Trish over there, I just broke up with my jackass boyfriend. Well, we never, like, got married or anything like that. But he's gone. And now I'm left by myself couch surfing with friends and slinging coffee at Starbucks while I pull my life back together."

Nancy studied Aen and wondered if she would manage enough stability in her life to make it through the entire six weeks of class. Nancy asked, puzzled, "So what you inspired you to sign up for a quilting class?" It seemed like a fair enough question. Aen wasn't going to spend quiet evenings at home hand sewing by a fireplace anytime soon.

"So, like," Aen started to explain, "I'm working on creating this new stage performance. It's about the life of my grandma, but reinterpreted in a new way. Like, from now. She's dead. And I thought I'd work on sewing, the way she did, to connect with her. But in this class I want to make some radical fabric I can hang on the stage. You know, so everyone can think about fabric, sewing and women's lives."

Nancy wasn't sure she followed Aen's thought process.

Aen added, "And, I'm showing what scum men are."

Nancy couldn't disagree with Aen on her last point.

"So," asked Nancy, "the work you want to create needs to be large enough to be seen on stage? Not small, like a typical one block quilt sampler?"

"Yeah," answered Aen. "My friend showed me about quilting. But I don't want to mess with fluffy pillow stuff in the middle. I want just big pieces of fabric. You know, like banners."

"Okay, I think I've got it," said Nancy. She could already see that her new students were going in different directions from what she planned. She was surprised at how many artists she encountered after living for such a short time in Albuquerque. It was similar to the number of would-be actors who wait tables in Los Angeles.

Nancy turned to the last two women seated at the table. She couldn't be sure, but she guessed the elderly woman next to Aen was in her eighties. She seemed quiet but good natured. She had waited patiently as everyone else had introduced themselves.

"Hello, I'm Bernice," said the woman. "I'm a photographer and I live with my daughter near the university. The galleries representing my work always ask me to find new ways to display my photos. You see, people don't appreciate plain old photography the way they used to."

Someone remarked, "That's too bad."

"Oh no," replied Bernice. "It's fine. After doing the same old stuff for so many years, I'm ready for a change myself." She added, "Keeps me young."

"How can we help?" inquired Nancy.

Bernice explained, "I read about photo transfers to fabric, then quilting and beading the images to embellish them. Sounded like fun, so I thought I would give it a try."

Nancy stopped to think about it. "Well," she answered truthfully, "I don't have any experience teaching that. But, if you're willing to experiment, we can see how it goes."

Bernice looked agreeable. She seemed like the kind of sunny person who appreciates the gift of each new day. Nancy would probably start researching photo transfer techniques the same night online.

Nancy turned to the last student, an outdoorsy and trim woman wearing no makeup who was probably in her forties. The woman might feel annoyed to be last, except she was too busy sending messages on her iPhone. Nancy guessed her to be a Type A personality.

Nancy cleared her throat to get the last student's attention.

"Does this class make quilts that look like these pictures?" asked the woman as she held up her iPhone. She made no effort to introduce herself. Nancy tried to peer at the image, but she struggled to view such a small picture on the device. How did younger people look at such small things all day?

The woman sensed Nancy's discomfort and took a larger iPad out of her bag. She quickly found the same website and shared the photos with the whole class.

Nancy explained they were looking at very advanced quilting techniques, involving the intricate piecing of complicated designs with sewing machines, and some designs involving sewing by a pre-programmed machine. Almost all of the photos looked more like paintings than traditional quilt designs. Some were closer to machine embroidery than quilting. She explained to the class the designs were done by computer programming for sewing machines.

"Isn't that cheating?" asked Trish, ever the school teacher.

"Not really," answered Nancy. She explained about a range of techniques that still constituted a hand-made quilt, although they definitely got into some gray areas about what is meant by the term original. She redirected her class's attention back to the basic patterns she passed around in the picture books.

"So we're not making quilts like the iPad pictures?" asked the obviously disappointed woman.

Nancy picked up the class roster and scanned it. "You must be Jill," she deduced.

"Oh yeah, I'm Jill," the woman echoed.

She introduced herself. "My husband and I just moved here from Santa Fe. I take yoga classes at the Higher Power Yoga Studio across the street and saw your flyer."

"We just bought a little farm in the North Valley," she said. "Like what the young woman was talking about earlier, farming in the valley. Anyway, I've been looking into different types of animals. Some of my neighbors raise really weird stuff."

"Oh yeah," spoke up Ann. "I see regular animals in the valley like chickens and goats. But also llamas, emu and even ostrich."

"Really?" asked Nancy.

"Stay away from the ostrich," warned Keisha. "My friend farmed some once. They are so mean."

Jill concurred. "Yeah, we have a young daughter. We decided we didn't want her around any animals, like ostrich, that could really hurt her, but we're thinking about getting sheep."

"Sheep?" asked Nancy.

"For the wool," answered Jill.

She went on to explain like Keisha, she was looking for something she could produce. She researched different types of fibers, but she didn't really find anything yet to spark her interest.

"You're trying to think of different types of yarn to make from the wool to decorate the fabric?" asked Nancy.

"Something like that," answered Jill. Somehow she wanted to find a way to apply wool fiber to a quilt.

Raleigh spoke up, "Well, you've either got to put it on it… or in it…, that's my motto," he said with a giggle.

"You rock," said Aen with approval.

"Now wait a minute," interjected Nancy. "Raleigh thought of something here. I was only thinking of how to turn the wool into yarn and use it to stitch the surface of the quilt for decoration."

Jill asked, "What else would you do with wool?"

Nancy went on to explain Amish quilts from the 1940's and earlier were often stuffed with wool batting in the middle.

Sometimes they even used cashmere fibers. Modern quilts relied primarily on cotton or synthetic blends for their batting, although wool was popular again.

"I could use wool for the stuffing in the center of quilts?" asked Jill, her eyes lighting up.

"I think the fibers must be treated or bonded together somehow," said Nancy. "But it's definitely worth researching."

The store was now full of interest and excitement. What a great start to Nancy's first quilt class. She breathed a sigh of relief. She felt like she would be successful as an entrepreneur. She started with the right stuff to run a quilt store.

Nancy told the students to take out notebooks and start drawing ideas or shapes to use as a quilt block pattern. She brought some pre-made pattern books if anyone got stuck but she hoped they could design their own ideas.

She watched with satisfaction as the students started to form into small working groups. Ann and Janice were already friends before attending the class. Being neighbors as well, they could work on their projects together between classes. Nancy sensed Ann bolstered Janice's confidence and self-esteem. Ann also went out of her way to talk with Trish, the newly divorced teacher and single parent. Nancy thought Ann must be an unusually compassionate person. Nancy remembered she didn't find an accountant yet in town and tax season would soon be upon her. She made a mental note to call Ann about her book keeping.

Aen was drawn to Raleigh's sense of humor. They leaned together over their notebooks laughing. The two probably drew dirty pictures together.

The other women talked among themselves. Nancy overheard Jill invite Trish to bring her son to see newly purchased chickens at her North Valley property. Their young kids would be close in age, even though the mothers were probably more than a decade apart.

Out of nowhere, Tompkins, the quilt shop cat, jumped into the middle of the table, surprising the entire group. He was so fat he struggled to get all the way up in one leap, but was quite happy to be the center of attention. He lulled in contentment as he got his belly scratched. It was odd. Tompkins was rather shy and tended to hide when anyone came into the store.

Nancy felt herself shiver as a cold breeze swirled around her. She looked at the group of students, but no one else seemed to notice. She definitely felt colder. The front door was closed and the heat turned up. As Nancy shivered more, she felt the hair on her arms start to prick up.

Nancy remembered a folk tale from her childhood. You knew lightning was about to strike when the hair on your arms stood straight up.

Nancy looked around the store again. Everyone else continued to chat and play with Tompkins. Why did she suddenly feel so eerie? Like there was extra energy in the room with her, but it was cold, not warming?

After the class was dismissed, and Nancy was finally home and tucked into bed, she decided the eerie cold feeling must be nerves. What else could explain such an odd sensation?

CHAPTER 8

Fay relaxed in the bored husband chair at the front of the quilt shop as Nancy tried to put together a new display for her large front picture window. Nancy knew she needed to create something alluring for the quilt shop. Valentine's Day was coming. She gathered together all of her bolts of red fabric, but try as she might, she couldn't seem to arrange them in any sort of artful display.

When she tried stacking the bolts of fabric, it looked as though they fell off the back of a truck into a pile. When she tried setting them up on their sides, it looked as though the front window was piled high with fabric bolts waiting to be put away. In frustration, she threw some bolts of fabric into the air, only to watch them fall together in a disorganized heap.

She sat down amid the pile and sighed.

"Do you want help?" asked Fay cheerfully.

Nancy answered, "I'm in desperate need."

Fay left and happily returned from her own store carrying a large fake tree and a bag of props. Making new arrangements always put Fay in the best of moods. Soon the two dug through the bag for ideas.

"I am so ready for spring," remarked Fay, which gave her inspiration. She found some flower pots, and then told Nancy to gather up sewing supplies and ribbons.

Under Fay's remarkable flair for decorating, they set up the bare tree and flower pots in the display window. Next Fay draped several shades of luscious silky red fabrics on the floor, around the base of the trees and flower pots. She found gauzy red fabric to drape from the tree branches, creating canopies of red. She tucked red floral fabrics into the insides of the flower pots.

Next the two women set up white birds in the tree. They took the sewing supplies, and made red and white ribbon flowers to attach to them. They stuck the sewing supplies with their faux flowers into waiting flower pots. Fay draped even more ribbons off the pots, the same way festive ribbons hang down from a May Pole.

They completed the design by hanging white ribbons, about a foot in length each, down from the ceiling, and hung sheer white fabric in the background. They completed the look by throwing white glitter on the red fabric on the floor. The whole scene was magical.

Nancy was stunned when she looked at the window display from the front sidewalk. Fay also gave her instructions about adding lighting to the tree. It would make the display more eye-catching in the daytime and quite dramatic at night.

Nancy marveled once again at Fay's ability to decorate. It was just the touch of drama her store needed. She couldn't wait to post photos online. She would start an archive of seasonal window displays. It helped her get in the mood for Valentine's Day.

As they cleaned up the last of their window display mess, they heard a yowl from Nancy's back office. Running into the room they found Tompkins rolling around on the floor.

"Does he get fur balls?" asked Fay.

"That cat has a bad tendency to eat everything—fur, plastic, old hamburgers from the dumpster behind Marconi's," answered Nancy.

Fay looked concerned. "You know dear, the exterminator sprayed yesterday. I wonder if Tompkins ate a poisoned bug or something?"

Both women peered over the cat. He continued to make noise and roll around on the floor.

"Do you know a veterinarian in the neighborhood?" asked Nancy. Of course, on the day Fay made her a fabulous new window display to lure in new customers, she needed to close her store to take Tompkins to the vet.

"Yes, dear. I have a wonderful vet on Lomas Avenue. And her father is a vet, too. But semi-retired..."

Suddenly Fay stood up straight and was speechless.

"What is it? Did you remember they are closed today?"

"No," answered Fay. She didn't explain any further.

The two women stood in silence for a moment. Fay suddenly faked a smile and said, "I could take Tompkins to the vet, dear. It's no trouble. No trouble at all, really." She added again, "Completely no trouble."

"What do you mean?" asked a perplexed Nancy. "You were starting to tell me about the vet's semi-retired father."

"Oh, that," replied Fay coyly. "Well, no worries. Should I bundle up Tompkins and be off? Don't you own an extra-large kitty carrier? Something with extra carrying handles?" She looked more closely at Tompkins. "Perhaps something with wheels?"

"There is something about the semi-retired father vet you are not telling me."

The two women faced off.

"Nothing to tell."

"Obviously there is."

"I saw him first," Fay whined.

Nancy thought for a moment. Tompkins spewed something green on the carpet and yowled again.

Recognition spread across Nancy's face. "Our Mystery Man is a veterinarian? A semi-retired vet?" That explained the look on Fay's face. Nancy hadn't see that look since the night they sat together at the Standard Diner and spotted the Mystery Man walking up the street. Fay mentioned that she knew him from somewhere, but, at the time, she couldn't figure out where.

The implication seeped in and Nancy felt joy swell into her heart. Maybe Tompkins chose good timing after all. While she swore off men, she still obviously needed to take her ailing cat to the vet.

Nancy was startled to hear new customers walk through the front door of her shop. Fay wore a huge smug smile. After all, Fay's fantastic new window display lured them off the street.

Nancy watched helplessly as Fay heaved the oversized cat into her arms, tottered a few steps under his hefty weight, and staggered toward the back door. As Nancy rushed to the front of the store to wait on her customers, she called out, "Do not think you are going to pick Tompkins back up from the vet. I need to be the one to get him!"

Fay gave a muffled reply as she went out the back door, "I'm sure the vet will want to talk with you about new nutritional guidelines. Perhaps a weight loss program."

The nerve of Fay.

****

The next quilting class would not be as stressful for Nancy to teach. She now understood what to expect, and found herself immersed in new research. She ordered the supplies for Bernice to work on her photo transfer project.

Jill's interest in using wool as batting for a quilt was exciting. She and Jill traded emails as they discovered new online research and tidbits to send to one another. Nancy had never paid much attention to batting before and had never contemplated trying to mill custom batting. She didn't know that small specialty fiber mills existed around the country which processed unique orders.

Nancy was intrigued to learn custom processing and blending could produce batting out of merino, cashmere, angora—which comes from a rabbit, mohair—which comes from a goat, and various other animals such as alpaca, llama, yak, buffalo, muskoxen, camel, beaver and even dogs and cats. Tompkins might prove himself valuable after all.

Batting could also be made from silk, soy silk, nylon, kelp, milk protein, hemp and bamboo. Many exotic fibers needed to be blended to stabilize them. Wool was a popular stabilizer. She learned it depended on the length of the fibers. For example, she found silk might work with camel hair.

Jill would have her hands full to figure out what blends make the most sense, but Nancy hoped Jill would develop a niche product. However, there was the question of what constituted organic and whether there was enough demand to pursue certification.

Nancy already offered to sell the batting Jill developed in her quilt store. It would be a huge opportunity for both of them. She started working on a potential marketing plan. She wanted to take Jill's product, or something similar, to a national audience before some larger retailer or distributor approached Jill. Nancy didn't want a competitor creating a knock-off product and marketing faster than her.

Exotic quilt batting was the silver bullet she searched for--some type of specialty she could market from her store. She began to think about other niche items she could sell, perhaps handmade fabrics or special types of embroidery threads. After all, she reasoned to herself, if someone spent months or years sewing a quilt, why not create a unique end product?

Nancy began to daydream about how wool could incorporate into quilting in general. She learned New Mexico boasted a long tradition of sheep and wool production, from Native American blankets to Spanish colonial embroidery, called Colcha. She read websites which talked about how Colcha became an endangered art form. While Colcha meant something different in places like Texas, in Northern New Mexico it referred specifically to a type of embroidery used on bedspreads, but not quilts. Traditionally Colcha yarn came from Churro sheep.

She also learned in her research the railroad built in the 1890's made hand embroidered goods less desirable, although Colcha enjoyed a short revival during the New Deal art programs, when classes were held. Some women formed a club to preserve Colcha in the Española Valley of Northern New Mexico. It gained additional interest in the 1960s at the annual Spanish Market in Santa Fe.

Nancy learned at some point the concept of quilts, as opposed to Colcha, was introduced, possibly during the Mexican occupation. Bright and heavy fabrics were used with contrasting colors. The women pieced together sections of weaving into a quilt instead of trying to weave a cloth into the entire length of a bedspread, then mix together different types of fabric, including denim. The quilts were stuffed with cotton or wool, and sometimes old rags. Usually the resulting heavy quilts were tied off with yarn instead of sewn together.

New Mexico quilts apparently were not decorative and never openly displayed. The family would cover the top of their beds with old sheets or Colcha bedspreads if they owned them. Nancy wondered if there was any history of combining Colcha stitching with a quilt. But so far, she found no evidence of it.

She was excited about the possibilities of wool fabric, yarn and batting in modern quilting. She had never considered wool batting before, even though she grew up in a cold Midwestern climate. She needed to experiment to find out how difficult wool and other fiber blends were to use in quilting. Could she stitch through two layers of wool cloth and thick batting? Could she use wool felting to create unique shapes and patterns? What kind of thread was appropriate? Her mind whirled with the implications.

Nancy felt like life finally went in her direction. She discovered exciting new avenues of research which she never would imagine if she didn't move to Albuquerque.

She let her mind wander to the vet pick up. She would finally talk with her Mystery Man. Enough time elapsed from her blind date to contemplate being attracted to a man. She decided any man who worked with animals must possess a kind heart. Unlikely he was rich, as vets don't earn much in general practice, but that was fine by her. She would settle for a stable man who was not neurotic.

Who was neurotic? She admitted she was jaded from her last encounter. Conflicting thoughts raced through her mind. Could she allow vulnerability again? Was it so long since she fell in love she didn't know how anymore?

She resolved to push her worries to the back of her mind.

****

Nancy hummed a happy tune to herself when she arrived at the vet's office. She would finally see her handsome Mystery Man again.

In the exam room she was greeted by an indifferent Tompkins. It reminded her of a joke-- What is the difference between a cat and a dog? If you put both a cat and a dog into boxes, when you return an hour later, the dog will be happy to see you.

Tompkins turned away from her and sauntered across the table to the vet. Of course, she didn't bring a pocket full of cat treats like him.

Nancy raised her eyes and gazed longingly into the Mystery Man's face. She now knew he sported blue eyes and a name tag labeled Dr. Bob Gill. She seemed at a loss for words as his deep, sexy voice prescribed the amount of food for Tompkins to eat. Fay was correct. It was time for the quilt shop cat to start a diet. She guessed the semi-retired vet was about her own age, which made Fay older than either of them.

Nancy felt a huge smile spread across her face.

"I'm glad to see you are happy about Tompkins' new Slim Cat diet," commented Dr. Bob. He was no longer the Mystery Man.

"Oh yes," she replied, startled. Once again, she was caught lost in thought. Perhaps not hearing the vet's instructions was a good excuse to call him back, because she didn't know about the particulars of the new diet he just outlined for Tompkins.

"We never found anything specifically wrong with Tompkins," Dr. Bob continued. "That's why we kept him for observation. He probably just ate something he shouldn't have."

"Probably," she agreed, smiling.

She observed Dr. Bob wasn't particularly tall, perhaps on the large end of medium. He was a little taller than her, which would make him around Fay's height. Fay might be the taller of the two, she thought happily to herself.

Nancy realized the good doctor stopped talking and was looking directly at her.

"You seem familiar," he said.

"I think you were in my quilt shop," she answered. "On Gold Street."

Nancy looked at Dr. Bob hopefully, but he remained perplexed.

Nancy added, "I'm next door to the Downtown Tea Shop and Gallery."

"Oh, yes!" exclaimed Dr. Bob.

Nancy was suddenly annoyed. Fay obviously talked with him when she brought in Tompkins for treatment. She invited him to stop by her store!

"Did Fay mention I'm still looking for fabric?" asked Dr. Bob.

"She did not," replied a petulant Nancy.

Dr. Bob explained he was in charge of putting together a garden show display for a weekend of workshops. He was running out of time to find table covers. Nancy was glad to help.

"Fay was quite nice and said she could help me put together something last minute for the show," continued Dr. Bob. "What a relief. I don't have any idea about that sort of thing. Fay said I should take a look at the window display at the quilt shop. She did the arrangement."

Nancy sniffed, "She did part of the work." She added, "Although I'm not really sure Fay has an eye for fabrics, per se."

Dr. Bob didn't seem to notice the last comment. He promised he would get by both their stores soon. She urged him to visit the quilt shop first, so she could show him her superior fabrics.

CHAPTER 9

Nancy left the vet with Tompkins, with just enough time to pick up dinner and eat while she prepared for her second night of quilting class. Fay lost no time in coming over to the quilt shop to ask about Dr. Bob, and how Tompkins was doing, of course. For his part, Tompkins showed no remorse. He already hunted Nancy's break area for morsels of dropped crumbs.

Fay still chatted with Nancy about Dr. Bob as her quilting students began to arrive in ones and twos. Fay waited until everyone assembled, then stood up to make an announcement. She described the gallery space in the tea shop next door. She invited the students to bring her their finished work at the end of class. She wanted to display the work at an upcoming ArtsCrawl, when the gallery would open late on for a First Friday event, and people from around the city could see their work.

All the students became excited. They applauded Fay as she left the store. Nancy was reminded of how helpful it was to have a supportive friend next door. She would be very gentle when the other woman realized Dr. Bob was both too young and too short for her.

The second session of quilting class started out orderly. Ann and Janice showed everyone their sketches of traditional quilt patterns. Nancy noted both designs were complicated. She kept silent. She didn't want to discourage the pair. She didn't yet have a sense about either student's sewing abilities.

Trish was thought getting fabric paint and making her own design to stitch. She was inspired by Bernice's photo transfer concept. Bernice hunted through her photo collection to find the right image to embellish with stitching.

Keisha talked about making a bold graphic pattern. Jill, who was focused on the potential for own batting in the middle, thought she might make quilt samples from solid fabric rather than worry about the design. She hoped to try different fiber blends and offered to share sample batting with the class. Raleigh wanted to create an abstract design with shades of white cloth, and use fusing tape to iron his project together. He would skip batting in the center or stitching the fabric.

Nancy looked around the class satisfied, but realized she almost forgot Aen.

Aen stood up and proudly held up her large sketch for the class to see. She had designed a banner for her upcoming performance. She waited patiently for feedback from the other students.

"Are they, umm, mushrooms?" asked Keisha.

"No," Aen replied.

"A row of trees?" guessed Jill.

"Nope," replied Aen.

"Just plain abstract art?" ventured Ann.

"No again," answered Aen.

"It's like a row of atomic bomb explosions," remarked a concerned Janice.

A smile spread across Raleigh's face. "Well, darlings," he announced, "We should see glorious explosions of some kind!"

"No..." mumbled Nancy, mostly to herself.

"They look like penises," said a small, frail voice. Bernice was correct and not self-conscious about it. Nancy guessed at her age, Bernice already saw about everything.

"Oh my God!" exclaimed a very embarrassed Keisha. "Are you, like, allowed to do that?"

Everyone in the class turned to Nancy to see what she would say. She realized that she had never encountered any such issues teaching college level anthropology. Perhaps she should have spent more time hanging around the art department. Those instructors were known for their off-beat thinking.

"Ahh..." she stalled for time.

"That's pretty pornographic," judged Ann.

"Don't you worry about offending your audience at your performance?" added Janice.

Nancy doubted Aen ever worried about being offensive. It was a rhetorical question of sorts.

"Aren't they too small?" asked Bernice.

Dead silence filled the room as everyone turned to look at the shrunken old woman with the sweet smile, until everyone burst out laughing, Raleigh loudest of all.

"Too small!" Raleigh repeated, laughing even harder.

Bernice waited patiently for quiet in the room again. "No offense," she said to Aen. "I'm not criticizing your design. I just wonder if the audience could see a row of so many penises that small." She added gently, "Why don't you make fewer, and make them larger? Everyone in the audience, even the back row, will be able to see them."

Aen turned her sketch back to herself and studied Bernice's suggestion. Nancy realized Bernice made a useful artistic suggestion.

"Bigger is much better," observed Raleigh.

Soon the class settled back down into the practical aspects of their designs. Nancy walked around the room and talked with each student about how to execute their work. Since only four weeks remained, everyone needed to work on their actual project by the following class.

Before the evening ended, everyone gathered together to discuss materials. Nancy located a good material for photo transfers. She thought it might work for painting as well. They talked about issues with cutting out geometric designs for those who chose to piece something together. She reminded them to look around their houses and find fabric scraps to recycle.

Keisha spoke up to tell the class where she located some fabric already. She lived in an apartment next door to a very cute guy. She spent weeks trying to get the nerve to initiate an actual conversation with him, but she could never think of the right thing to say. She always smiled and ducked into her apartment whenever she saw him.

"But you're good looking," observed Janice, with admiration.

"You've got it going on, girlfriend," added Raleigh.

"I don't know why I'm suddenly shy around him," remarked Keisha truthfully. "I don't usually have this problem, but he is just so, I don't know." She searched for the right description. "Amazing. He isn't like other guys I know."

Keisha went on to explain when she came home last week; she found a bag of Goodwill donation clothes in front of his door, so she took it. She planned to make her project out of his give-away clothes. She positively beamed at the thought.

"Do you think it will bring me good luck in meeting him?" she asked the class brightly.

"Makes you a world class stalker," answered Aen.

Jill came to Keisha's defense. "She didn't steal the clothes from inside his apartment. She only took what he threw away anyway and will recycle it. Very eco-friendly of her."

"You could make a voodoo doll," observed Trish, startling her classmates with the venom in her usually mild voice.

"Oh Trish, honey," chimed in Ann. "You and Aen were burned so badly in love. Let this young lady have her sweet dreams about her cute guy. I remember what it was like to want to be near a young fellow so badly I would want to just touch his shirt. To feel the fabric and know he wore it."

"I still have those thoughts about young men," chirped Raleigh happily.

Aen was unconvinced and spoke directly to Keisha. "You should know the truth. The sooner, the better. Men suck."

"Only if you are lucky," continued an undeterred Raleigh.

"Come to my performance," countered Aen. "You'll see how it really is with men. They are scum."

The arguments about men in tonight's class mirrored Nancy's own inner turmoil. Just last week she would side with Trish and

Aen, believing men were best left alone. They lead directly to heartache. Now she found herself rooting for Keisha to meet her prized young man, and experience love, open and innocent of how much a divorce can hurt.

Maybe, she realized, she was projecting her own hopes on Keisha. Could she really ever approach love again with an open heart, with a Beginner's Mind?

Nancy never really understood the concept of a Beginner's Mind on an emotional level before. However, looking around her class, she realized she faced a choice. She could be as bitter as Aen, or she could embrace love as if she were young Keisha.

Nancy failed to contemplate the amount of immaturity that can go along with juvenile love.

CHAPTER 10

It was a quiet Sunday afternoon. Nancy made preparations to close shop when Fay and Dr. Bob walked through her front door laughing together. She stared at them in a less than friendly manner, noting that she was correct; Fay and Dr. Bob were almost the same height. Dr. Bob stood maybe an inch or two over Fay.

"We came to pick out fabric, dear," said Fay in a sickly sweet voice. She actually found the nerve to reach out, hook her arm under Dr. Bob's, and pull him away from Nancy.

"You've already been to Fay's store?" asked a hurt Nancy, directly to Dr. Bob.

"Um, yes," he replied sheepishly. He looked caught in the middle and seemed to search his mind for some sort of explanation. It didn't seem to dawn on him that showing preference for one store over the other would cause problems.

"Well, of course dear, he stopped at the tea shop first," chimed in Fay, grabbing Dr. Bob's arm more tightly. "He met me several months ago—so we go way back. Just like old friends."

The fact that Fay could not identify Dr. Bob from the window of the Standard Diner less than a month ago seemed to elude her mind.

Nancy turned her attention back to Dr. Bob.

"So," she asked him, "Did you find anything interesting at Fay's store?"

It was a test of sorts.

"Um, well, no, not really," muttered Dr. Bob apologetically.

Nancy gave a smile of triumph.

Fay interrupted. "What this good doctor needs is fabric to cover tables at the upcoming plant and garden expo over at the fairgrounds."

"I now recall coming in here before to look at fabrics," admitted Dr. Bob.

"Was the selection too small?" inquired Fay. "Why don't we try one of those big fabric stores with more choices?"

"This is fine. I thought I needed green fabrics, but I don't know. I get confused when I look at this stuff. Fay, you said you could coordinate something for me."

"You're helping to run the expo?" inquired Nancy.

"Actually," answered Dr. Bob, "I'm just coordinating the display for the xeric gardeners."

"So you're a gardener yourself?" asked Fay with delight.

Dr. Bob started to shift uncomfortably in of Fay's clutches. She immediately sensed his discomfort, and with her typical good manners, gently let go of his arm. She proceeded to make small talk to put him at ease.

"You must tell us more about gardening," cooed Fay. "I know my yard could use some help. I think it just looks so drab these days. Nothing to brighten it up, just a plain old lawn. Would you advise me about adding lovely flowering bushes, like Azaleas, Hydrangeas or Forsythias?"

Nancy noted Fay looked very proud of her ability to use botanical language. Nancy couldn't differentiate one plant from another, let alone remember the names of shrubs with flowers off the top of her head.

"Well," said Dr. Bob, searching carefully for his next words. "I really don't have much expertise in that area."

"Gardening doesn't include bushes?" asked a clearly disappointed Fay.

"My area of study," explained Dr. Bob, "is native plants. I tend to focus on xeriscaping."

Nancy interjected, "He doesn't like people who waste a lot of water keeping a big fancy lawn alive in the desert, or plant bushes with silly flowers that don't belong here. He is obviously quite concerned about the planet and we don't run out of water in Albuquerque."

Nancy gave Fay a huge, smug smile.

Nancy didn't make an environmentally conscious decision about her own yard. She didn't use much water, but more out of neglect than choice. When she bought the house, the yard was basically dirt, and she hadn't done anything to fix it yet. She was amazed to move to this part of the country and find when a yard was empty; it could stay empty for a long time. Literally. Nothing much would grow in the bare dirt until periodic rains came, or late summer moisture. She was warned by the end of the summer rains, she could find weeds in her yard taller than herself. One of her neighbors lent her a couple books on xeriscaping. She still needed to find plants to fill her yard.

But, as was often the case with Nancy, she started research, but never progressed to any actual physical work.

A hurt Fay returned to the conversation. "You know, I always do intend to do something about my lawn. I haven't figured out what. Most of my neighbors in Country Club still grow grass and beautiful huge cottonwood trees. That's part of what makes the neighborhood so special. I shudder to think what would happen if everyone poured a ton of rocks into their front yards."

Many homeowners in Albuquerque embraced ZEROscaping: ugly white rocks dumped in the place where a lawn might be.

Nancy traveled to some other areas of New Mexico, like Santa Fe and Taos, and noticed they worked competently with native plants and avoided a gravel pit for a front yard.

"It doesn't have to be that way," said Dr. Bob. "Come to the expo and see some ideas for using indigenous plants."

"Can you help us with that?" asked Nancy. "I have an empty yard and want to figure out what I should plant." She added, "I just moved here from Indiana and don't know about local landscape."

She batted her eyes at him.

Fay upped the stakes. "Would you be so kind as to stop at my house to take a look at my yard? I could make us some tea or dinner."

"I think I need help even more," interjected Nancy. "My yard is bare dirt. Perhaps we could have drinks?"

"Don't you need to finish the inside of your house? I believe you said you had all you could handle with your kitchen repairs."

"That was before I knew I would meet someone with plant expertise."

"No, I'm fairly sure you don't have time to take on a yard this year, and it would be so rude to waste this poor man's time."

"What? You think I waste people's time?"

"I'm just saying it would make more sense to start at my house."

Fay turned to Dr. Bob and asked, "Right?"

As the conversation escalated, both women failed to notice Dr. Bob edge closer to the front door. He looked at his watch and announced, "I'm really sorry to run off so quickly, but I must be going now. Thanks for the conversation, ladies."

Both women stood quietly.

The store seemed totally empty. A dark cloud settled upon the women, and they both stared into the bleakness.

"See what you did?" asked Fay.

"What I did?" answered back Nancy.

"Yes, you."

"I am not the one who scared him off with a big waste of a lawn."

"Why you!" exclaimed Fay.

The two of them squared off with each other.

"He was in a wonderful mood after looking at my store and talking with me," sniffed Fay.

"Bored," said Nancy, under her breath.

"What did you just say?" yelled Fay.

"I said," replied Nancy angrily, "he was probably just being polite to his elder. Glad the two of you can see eye-to-eye."

Both women's faces were bright red. The temperature in the room seemed to rise.

"Is there a reason for you to be in my store?" asked Nancy, with cruelty.

"Yes, there is," Fay snapped back. She turned around slowly, at a loss for why she was still there until she spotted the picture window.

"I am here," she yelled, "to take back my window display items! Because," she added for emphasis, "they are obviously not appreciated."

She stomped to the window, pulled down the white sheer fabric hanging from the ceiling, and proceeded to extract her tree and birds. With her hands full, she announced, "I'll be back for my flower pots. Please get them ready for me."

Nancy responded in her own fit of anger, "Don't bother coming back! I'll pile your precious flower pots by your front door." She stood with her arms crossed as her front door slammed. She took apart the rest of her window display, lining the pots in a couple of neat rows.

She soon realized the floor of her window display was a hopeless tangled mess of fabric and ribbon pieces. She felt inadequate to fix it, except she wasn't about to give Fay the satisfaction of seeing her fall apart.

She vowed she would make her own window display, but not today. She would stay up late tonight just to clean up the mess.

Her front door opened and Theresa M wandered in.

"Hi, my café is closed already, and I thought I would stop by," she said warmly. She noticed tears stream down Nancy's face and asked, "Are you okay?"

"Yes," replied Nancy, but she didn't look it.

"The Valentine's Day display got to you?" inquired Theresa M politely.

"There is no such thing as love," answered the other woman.

"Wow," said Theresa M.

She walked to the chair and sat down quietly to give Nancy time to compose herself.

Nancy gathered up all her fabric and ribbons when Theresa M spoke again, "Actually, I stopped by to ask for your help."

"Really?"

"Yeah, it's for my friend Keisha. You know, taking your quilting class."

"Is she having trouble with her project?" a focused Nancy asked. No matter what happened, she was a good teacher.

"Yeah," replied Theresa M.

Nancy wiped her eyes. She stopped to think about Keisha's work. "Is she having trouble with those fabric scraps? You know, the ones she found in a bag outside her apartment? In front of the cute guy's apartment door? It can be very difficult to use strange types of fabric you are not familiar with. She might get slick polyester or something equally difficult in her bag. Some type of fabric which doesn't sew well."

"That's it."

"Keisha has a problem with polyesters?" asked Nancy.

"No," said Theresa M, "the bag."

"There's a problem with the bag?"

"Yes."

Nancy began to realize this conversation would take a while. She put aside the fabric and ribbons, and then sat down on her window display. She calmed down and became ready to listen.

Theresa M began to outline the bag problem. Keisha came up with a design for her project, then proceeded to cut up the clothing from the bag to make her quilt block. She figured out a great design with different colored squares of fabric. She found a wonderful variety of textures. She even cut off the buttons from the clothes to make cool accents.

But then, a couple days later, she ran into Cute Guy in the hallway. He told her he borrowed some clothes from his brother. He washed the clothes and left them in the hallway in front of his door for his brother to pick up, but someone stole the bag! He wondered if Keisha saw anyone suspicious in the building.

"Wow," was all Nancy said.

"Yeah," answered Theresa M. "She was really bummed out because it was her first conversation with the guy of her dreams."

"Did she tell Cute Guy what happened to his brother's clothes? You know, come out and tell the truth?"

"Um, no. She texted me while she talked with him. I thought we should ask you."

"Figures," said Nancy.

Nancy realized she was in no condition to help Keisha figure out her dilemma, and explained this as best she could. She decided what they needed to do was talk about it together in a place away from Gold Street where everyone could think.

Did the two young women want to visit the plant expo? Nancy wouldn't attend with Fay obviously, although she wanted to see Dr. Bob again. She was surprised when Theresa M readily agreed. She and Keisha knew friends with farms and greenhouses who would exhibit there and were thinking about going anyway.

CHAPTER 11

Nancy sensed that her life was now on some sort of strange downward spiral. It was as if her argument with Fay in her store had unleashed some type of negative force in her life. She did not believe in the Law of Attraction or any other such nonsense. However, if she was the type of person who believed in astrology, which she most certainly did not, she would figure she entered a bad moon rising. Somehow all the planets began to align against her.

She was not surprised when she got a phone call a couple days later from one of her students. Ann and Janice started to become overwhelmed in quilting class. Both felt like failures because they struggled to piece together basic patterns while the artists in the class created original masterpieces. Ann called to inquire if a more basic quilting class would be held without artists. Nancy didn't think it was possible to arrange in Albuquerque.

Nancy calmed Ann down and talked her into stopping by the quilt shop with Janice. She would sit down with them and figure out what was wrong with their projects.

They arrived the next day. Both still seemed discouraged, although Janice seemed to take it the hardest of the two.

"I'm just no good at this stuff," said Janice in a dejected voice.

"What are you talking about?" asked Ann. "You have decorative pillows and other cute crafts all over your house that you made over the years. Didn't you tell me you sewed baby blankets and outfits for each of your kids?"

"I don't know any hand sewing. And it seems like such a long time ago…"

Nancy observed deep creases on Janice's forehead and a long frown. Her sadness seemed much deeper than a quilt pattern.

"Are you okay?" asked an equally concerned Ann.

"I don't know what it is," answered Janice. "Menopause is

starting to take its toll on me. I don't sleep right and those darn hot flashes."

"Why don't you try some of the pills I take?" asked Ann. "They really seem to help."

"I have to tell you," said Nancy, "I'm in favor of whatever eases the symptoms. I was on meds when all those nasty reports came out about hormone replacement therapy. I went off for a few weeks and terrorized all of my students. I was much happier after I went back on, although I didn't keep taking them forever, just until the worst passed."

"I don't think they would cure me," said Janice.

The women laid out pieces of fabric for Nancy to examine and give suggestions about quilt patterns. Nancy searched through her pre-made pattern books until she came across simple traditional designs. Nancy always favored the classics anyway. Most of the patterns represented traditional symbols, such as important occasions or each of the fifty states. Each state received a unique pattern, in the same way a state gets a specific bird or flower.

Janice picked up the book and flipped through some of the patterns. "I lived in half these places. I thought I would know by now where I want to live when I grow up."

She made a half-hearted attempt to laugh.

"Oh, honey," said Ann. "That's what's getting you down. Our kids are about to leave home. Maybe you feel a little lost? I'm so busy at work I tend to forget, but you're Super Mom. Why, how many times did you help me with cookies for my own kids' classrooms or assist with their homework? Your house is a second home to them. One that's much cleaner and more organized."

Janice set the book down. "I used to be on top of everything, but now it doesn't seem the same. I don't feel my old spirit. Mike points out to me that I'm not keeping up with chores the way I used to and don't look well-kept anymore. I put on weight and cut my hair shorter."

Ann and Nancy exchanged annoyed looks.

"Your husband said you look bad?" asked Nancy.

"I don't blame him," answered Janice. "See the wrinkles on my face? I'm starting to get deep crow lines."

Ann could no longer contain herself. "Your lines are from frowning and caused by listening to Mike! What does he know? He must go through man-o-pause himself. Men get their time of life, too. Don't listen. You look great."

Ann randomly flipped the quilt pattern book open and started to thumb through the pages. "Stop me when you see something."

"Stop," said Janice. "I like this design."

Nancy peered over Janice's shoulder. "That's a Double Wedding Ring. It's beautiful. However, circles are rather difficult for beginners. I recommend starting with triangles and squares."

"But maybe if I worked harder at the wedding thing I would be a better person," said Janice. The comment didn't seem directed at quilts in particular.

"Enough of this talk," reprimanded Ann.

"Isn't it funny to remember what we thought marriage would be like when we were young?" asked Nancy.

"Oh, yeah, I was totally into it," said Janice. "I played wedding with my dolls all the time."

"What else did you dream about?" asked Nancy.

"Oh, just silly things," replied Janice.

"No, really, come on," said Ann. "Tell us about other things that you thought you would do when you grew up. I thought I would be the first woman president."

"You still could be," remarked Nancy. "We still haven't elected one yet."

"Ummm," said Janice, searching for words. "Honestly, I spent a lot of time picturing myself as a mom. My own mother was fantastic and I always looked up to her. I thought it would be great to start a family. Does that sound lame?"

"Would your mother be happy to see you this sad?" asked Ann.

The other two women gave her space to mull over her mother.

"I guess you're right," answered Janice. "My mom always encouraged me to do my best. She thought I could accomplish anything. She would tell me to put on a happy face and I was sure to feel better."

"That's the spirit," said Ann.

"Right," said Nancy.

"I can get back on track with my family," said Janice with new energy. "Just the other day I thought I haven't cleaned out the pantry in a while."

It wasn't exactly the answer Nancy wanted. What did she expect? Was it wrong of Janice to enjoy being a housewife?

Nancy realized she was in no position to judge. What did she know about successful relationships anyway? She didn't know how to make a long-term partnership work.

Nancy pressed the quilt pattern book into the women's hands and gave them specific advice about how to proceed with their projects as she bundled them out the door.

****

Despite a small success cheering up Janice, gloom still hung over the shop. Nancy looked forward to teaching her next class even less when she received a phone call from Bernice's daughter. Bernice had contracted the winter flu and would spend the night in the hospital. While her daughter tried to remain upbeat, they both knew that flu is dangerous to someone in their eighties with frail health. Even after Bernice was due back home the doctor suggested she shouldn't be around the public for a while. She wondered how long it would be before they saw the gentle old woman again.

A bad vibe was definitely in the air. Aen called and said that her show was would open in a couple weeks, maybe sooner, and she didn't make her banners. Nancy could point out she didn't plan very well in advance. Of course her project wasn't done. They only completed two classes, and Aen chose an impossibly huge undertaking.

As she mulled the situation over, she realized Aen was unlikely to finish sewing one banner in time, even if she used a machine instead of hand stitching. She talked with her a while and heard her friend's attempt to teach her to hand sew didn't go very well. Nancy doubted she could do much better.

Normally she could problem-solve such difficult situations. Why was her mind a dark blank these days? Her third quilting class, just before Valentine's Day, would be a challenge at best.

At the end of the day Nancy sat down at the front of her store to contemplate the mess she made of her life. She wasn't sure what she thought owning a business would be like, but it wasn't this.

She never realized it would be so hard to keep going. She began to realize she sacrificed quite a bit to start her own company from scratch. She might earn more money working at the local hardware store. Or she could buy a retirement condo in Florida with Fay's friend Bunny. Okay, not Bunny, since she and Fay still wouldn't speak. Living in Albuquerque she managed to make and lose a new best friend in less than a year.

Maybe she should take a much longer look in the mirror before embarking on a reckless adventure, and moving cross country. Was she too old for this? She knew a life of stability back home with long-time friends. Life back home was dependable — if lonely in the love department.

She was well respected in her old field. People knew her and would seek out her opinion. People invited her to present at conferences. She should start a second career writing books or consulting. Instead, she worked long hours as a shop clerk. She hadn't done a job this menial since high school.

She thought back over her day. She restocked bins of threads, lined up rows of pre-packaged quilt binding, and shelved bolts of fabric.

Was this the final result of an advanced degree? Would her tombstone read here lays our favorite stock girl?

Self-pity got the best of her.

Finally she asked herself the question she avoided for weeks — was it time to cut her losses and close the quilt shop?

Nancy didn't think of herself as a quitter. She often prided herself on her tenacity and ability to see almost any project through to completion. However, the store started to feel like a failure. She calculated more numbers about her cash flow; despite her class, the new website, and some marketing efforts, she still didn't generate a positive cash flow.

How much time would it take? She already blew through her inheritance. It seemed disrespectful to the memory of her parents to lose their hard-earned savings in a failed business venture. At the same time, she recalled her parents always wanted her to be happy. Even when she divorced at a relatively young age in a time when people didn't usually do that, her parents stood behind her decision. Her mother always told her there was no reason to let her life go to pot.

She tried to imagine her parents standing in front of her. Why could she see the past so vividly in her fainting spells, but not now? She squinted to concentrate harder. She even walked to her own computer to stare at the monitor. Nothing happened like the travel company.

She sat down by her cash register. She should go through the numbers more logically. Her stomach churned. She couldn't look at them again. The balances started to creep up on her credit cards and soon she would be at her limits. The only next step seemed to be to cash out her retirement savings early. She was warned not to do it as she would incur huge penalties, but she ran out of other options. Was she even more foolish to stay open, and throw good money after bad?

When Nancy locked her store that evening, baby blue skies and a pink sunset streaked across the skyline. Nancy filled with utter annoyance. Why couldn't it rain? Why was the New Mexico sky so relentlessly sunny? She was ready for dark winter clouds and a freak thunderstorm. Definitely something involving a whole lot more gloom. She never imagined endless blue skies could get on a person's nerves so badly in the middle of winter.

Nancy knew, however, she found her metaphorical Heart of Darkness when she found herself huddled alone in the booth of a Cracker Barrel restaurant beside a freeway. She ignored the happy conversations of the families situated around her.

She always ate at Cracker Barrel on the road. She liked the comfort of their familiar food. It never failed to remind her of home.

She corrected herself. It brought back warm memories of her old life which slipped away in Indiana. Did she want to go back? She didn't own many things anymore. She cleared out the farmhouse before she left, and gifted the family heirlooms to nieces and nephews. She wouldn't pass anything on. She knew she couldn't go home again.

There was still time to hit the open highway. Maybe she didn't go far enough west. The coast offered beautiful oceans and endless beaches. Some days she missed the water in the desert.

Really, what reasons did she have to stay?

She told herself she didn't need love. Men were time wasters anyway. She certainly didn't need happy students. They already paid their class registration. She was not about to give them refunds. Most importantly, she didn't need friends.

Friends are people who just build you up only for the pleasure of tearing you back down. Who needs that in life? She could be perfectly happy in a strange city by herself. Just add some food and maybe a dozen bags of candy from the Old Country Store, a couple helpings of dessert and she would be fine. Good thing Cracker Barrel didn't serve alcohol.

Nancy picked up her menu and began to read the selections. She never developed a taste for classic Southern cooking. Therefore, dishes like turnip greens, fried okra, deep fried catfish, breakfast grits, and particularly pinto beans, held no appeal for her.

She scanned the dinner section with pure joy when she found Midwestern cooking: foods she had not seen in months—smoked country ham, chicken-n-dumplings, homemade beef stew and a delectable hash brown casserole. She could smell melted cheese already. She debated about whether she preferred a dessert of double fudge Coca-Cola cake or baked apple dumpling with pecan streusel. She would order them both.

The quilt shop owner experienced her first delight in days when dinner was finally served. She inhaled warm aroma from a plate of meatloaf topped with tomato sauce, green beans, mashed potatoes with gravy, and her ultimate favorite—macaroni and cheese. Yes, life would get better.

She took a large fork full of pasta and inspected it closely. Nowhere on the menu did she see the words green chile. It was as if the management never heard of the stuff. She slowly stuck her loaded fork of macaroni and cheese into her mouth to savor the richness of... a mushy and tasteless texture.

Wait a minute. The taste was not what Nancy expected.

What happened to her?

She took another bite. Perhaps the first was simply an adjustment. She needed to reacquaint her taste buds with good, old fashioned cooking. Did she permanently harm her sensory systems?

She rolled the pasta around inside her mouth, but it was no use. The thrill was simply gone. The bland food didn't taste right anymore. She ate her green beans, picked at the potatoes, and managed to swallow about half of the meatloaf, but she could not enjoy her meal. She decided to skip dessert. She wasn't up for any more disappointments.

Nancy looked around the restaurant, filled primarily with travelers from the highway. People made a quick stop before they got back into their cars and drove to another place. What was she doing here? She didn't belong to this tourist crowd. She chose to live Downtown because of the great local restaurants. The area supported the kind of place mostly known to people who lived there.

It was time to go home.

CHAPTER 12

Nancy stayed late at the store, telling herself she should catch up on work. Well, it wasn't quite true. The only task she managed to accomplish was additional worry about her finances.

Once Gold Street finally went dark she locked up. Luckily the weather was mild. Night is particularly cold in the desert. She wrapped up in a jacket against the night chill.

She slowly made her way across the street to the travel company. Silence greeted her from the window. All the office equipment was turned off.

What was she expecting?

She tried to reassure herself another fainting episode wasn't a good idea anyway. She was playing with fire. What if she hit the ground when she passed out this time?

She wasn't willing to entertain the notion her visions might be caused by anything but a fainting spell.

On the next block a group of kids opened the door of a lounge bar. Music and light spilled on to the street. She watched them laugh together. A bouncer drifted outside to stand under a street sign. He lit a cigarette and nodded in her general direction. When the bar door closed again, leaving the street in blackness, she found herself watching the dull glow of the tip of his smoke. He moved it around slowly. She assumed would be stand out there most of the night.

Why was she loitering in the darkness?

The wind kicked a brown leaf up the street. Nancy watched it roll away into the black of night. She was looking for the answers to her problems. Instead, she only saw emptiness.

****

Nancy assumed her third quilting class would be a challenge and she was right. The bad vibe continued to hang over her store and infect her students. She tried to make the best of it. Everyone immediately missed the wonderful energy of Bernice, who was somewhat recovered, but stuck at home. Keisha didn't arrive until the last fifteen minutes of class and didn't bring her project with her.

Nancy coaxed Ann and Janice along in their designs, although they didn't look happy about it. They both muttered under their breath as they wrestled with geometric shapes of fabric.

Jill continued to research creating batting out of wool and other blends of exotic fibers. She seemed stumped as to whether she should buy sheep or continue researching for awhile. Did she want to experiment with unusual animals? She and Trish discussed it.

Trish explained to the class she tried painting fabric squares for her project, but didn't think they turned out very well. The paints displayed a tendency to bleed or run, which made the resulting picture too abstract to quilt stitch.

Aen unfurled empty rolls of fabric for the class to contemplate how she might get banners done. She began to panic about her upcoming performance.

Worst of all, for Nancy, was Raleigh. She forgot how close he and Fay were. He looked rather peevishly at Nancy and refused to say much in class. She felt guilty about the fight with Fay. It was the first time she saw Raleigh quiet or in a bad mood.

Never did a couple hours go by so slowly. Nancy wondered if she should cancel class instead of endure the agony of minutes ticking by. She could stay home in bed for the next few days, except she couldn't hire anyone else to run the store for her.

Who invented a holiday as sadistic as Valentine's Day? Sure, it might be great for married women such as Janice and Ann. Then again, maybe not. It was worse for people in committed relationships. Some of them couldn't look forward to improvement the next year.

Nancy surveyed her store as her class toiled on. She gave up on assembling a new fancy display for her picture window to rival Fay's decorating ability. Instead she placed a stool in the window, unrolled a bolt of red fabric to cover it, and placed a faded plastic cherub statue she found at the thrift store on top. She liked to think Raleigh merely was cold when he paused in front of the display and shuddered.

She liked to tell herself she discovered minimalist design, and she didn't need all those frilly knick knacks her tea shop neighbor used everywhere. She could do fine by herself.

Except she knew she was lying to herself. She couldn't make a window display like Fay. She felt the absence of her friend every day, but still wasn't willing to swallow her pride and open her heart to her neighbor again.

At the end of the evening, as the class slowly shuffled out the front door, they heard yelling down the street. Everyone stopped and gathered to look. Nancy recognized Heather, George's niece, in front of an empty space with a for rent sign. She only recently became licensed to work in her uncle's real estate business. Nancy figured she was barely out of college.

"But you already signed a lease," said Heather in a strong voice.

Replied a short man, "That was before you tricked me."

"Nobody tricked anyone," countered the young realtor. "You saw the space, you inspected everything yourself, and you know everything is in working order. Then you signed a lease. You can't break it now."

"I didn't know you would trick me!" The man yelled again. In the light of the store signs Nancy saw his face flame red. "I want my security deposit back. This is fraud."

In concern for Heather's safety the students gathered around her. Nancy took up the rear with her cell phone ready to dial the police.

"Is there a problem?" asked the ever practical Ann.

"These people are frauds!" the man repeated. "This young lady told me everything was in order with this vacant space. But I hired contractors for the last week and nothing works right."

"You are responsible for hooking up your utilities and getting the space ready for your store," answered petulant Heather.

"But I can't!" yelled the distressed man. "I hired every decent contractor in this town I can get my hands on to look at this space. Nobody can figure out what you people did to the wiring! It's impossible! It's like you have ghosts."

"Oh, come now."

"I can't open a business in that space and I want my deposit back. I'm going to call the Attorney General if I need to."

From behind, Nancy heard a soft voice, "Heather knows she can't rent to him."

Nancy about jumped out of her skin. Where did Jane come from this late at night? She couldn't remember the Cosmic Travel & Tour Co. staying open after dark. Creepy.

Jane walked up quietly to Heather and the irate man. She stated, "Sir, if you'll go talk to George at the real estate office in the morning I'm sure he'll be happy to let you out of your lease and refund your deposit. There has obviously been a mistake."

"There was no mistake!" Heather now did the screaming.

The man seemed content with Jane's advice. He realized nothing was to be gained by continuing the argument. He stomped off into the night.

"What do you think you are doing?" demanded an annoyed Heather.

"What are you doing?" answered Jane back. "Heather, I'm sure your uncle explained to you can't rent the stores on this block to men."

"That's against the law!" cried Heather. "They repeated it to us again and again at real estate school." She said her words slowly, as if Jane were daft in the head. "Discrimination is illegal. I could lose my license over this. I must rent to men."

"But you can't," replied Jane simply.

With that, Jane disappeared into the darkness as quietly as she first appeared.

Heather stood with her hands on her hips. She flicked her long blond hair in annoyance. It took her a few moments to register that the quilt class stood together on the sidewalk to stare at her.

She turned to the class. "Know anyone who wants to rent a vacant store on Gold Street?"

"Can we look?" piped up Keisha.

"Sure, why not?" answered back the realtor. "I'm standing out here in the middle of the night anyway. I'm supposed to be a commercial broker. We don't work nights."

Heather stomped into the vacant store and gasped in surprise when she flicked all of the lights on. The entire space lit up brightly. "See Jane," she started to say, but looked around sheepishly and remembered Jane had already left. "Everything works fine," Heather said to no one in particular.

The class wandered through the empty space. The layout was very similar to the quilt shop, except for an extra row of windows on the east wall. It gave Nancy new perspective. This was how she started out a few short months ago, with only an empty space and a dream. Now she ran a full quilt shop and taught a class. Nancy never thought about how far she had come in such a short time.

Raleigh came over to Nancy and gave her a hug. "So this is what it's like? Starting something new?" He added with a wink, "I'm always into something new—particularly when it involves a group. Yes, extra special when it's an entire group."

"What kind of store would you open Raleigh?" Nancy asked a bit too loudly. Everyone seemed to stop and wait for his answer.

"Oh, darlings," replied Raleigh, "I am not into long term commitments."

"But I would rent to you," declared Heather. She added under her breath, "I don't care what Uncle George and spacey Jane say."

"I suppose this would be my studio," he answered. "I do like the windows, though I'm not usually up to see the sun rise. But what artist could afford a space this nice? That's why I work in a warehouse."

Ann looked around. "It's great to enjoy so much room, but my little CPA firm is fine in the Sunshine office building. I don't know what rent like this costs, but I'm sure it's a lot more than my cozy little office."

"Yes," Heather confirmed.

"I would rock out," declared Aen.

"How would you pay the rent?" inquired Janice.

"Whatever," answered Aen.

No landlords in their right mind would sign a lease with Aen in her current condition. She was lucky to secure three nights of theater space for her upcoming performance.

Keisha spoke up, her eyes suddenly gleaming, "I would open a store." The room seemed to glow more brightly.

"What kind?" asked Jill beside her.

Nancy wondered if Jill thought of the same idea as Keisha, opening her own store? Nancy started to panic. She hoped Jill would stick to her wholesale manufacturing business plan of producing fiber products. She already discovered several ideas about retailing them online. What if Jill decided to open her own competing store instead? It would be located near the quilt shop. Soon her mind was put to ease.

Jill commented, "I can't imagine running a store myself. You sit around all day and wait for people to show up. Yuck. I want to work with my hands. Didn't you say the same thing Keisha?"

"Yeah," answered Keisha, "but I don't know. I thought I wanted to make something, except I like my job at the mall selling clothes. Well, kind of. The stuff they sell is mostly boring. I would like to sell different clothes. I don't want people to all look the same."

"Cool," commented Trish. "I can never decide what I would do if I wasn't a school teacher. You always think of such good ideas, Keisha."

"You're so right," seconded Janice, looking lost. Nancy noticed sadness in her eyes. She continued, "You're young Keisha. You have your whole life ahead of you. You can decide to do anything."

"You can start new stuff when you're old," countered Keisha. "Just look at how old Nancy is and she opened her own store."

"Thanks," said Nancy. She wasn't upset because Keisha made a good point.

"What would you do?" asked Trish.

Janice answered, "Oh, I haven't thought about anything in particular. I don't have any special skills."

"Come on," prodded her friend Ann. "You and Mike talk about his retirement and how you'll find something new. Why not open a store?"

Janice shook her head no, but she clearly contemplated the idea. "I can't really do anything," she concluded.

"You can open an organizing business," declared Raleigh.

"What?" said several people in unison.

"Sure," replied Raleigh. "You talk about that kind of stuff all the time in class."

It was clear to Nancy Janice never thought about her own competencies in a long time. Raleigh was on to something.

"He's right," remarked Ann excitedly. "Janice, you moved, like, a zillion times. I'm an organized person, but you are way, way better than me. You create actual systems for keeping track of things, labeling, and getting rid of extra stuff. You know where to buy great containers really cheap and how to make them look good in your house. You don't use a bunch of ugly plastic bins. You find gorgeous trunks, fantastic old suitcases, vintage hat boxes, baskets with lids and fabric covered shoe boxes. You arrange them so stylishly on your selves and around every room. I am always amazed at your house."

Janice seemed to dismiss her friend's comments, but the room glowed even more brightly. "Oh, it's nothing. It's the military way. My father was an officer and my mother taught me how to move all the time. I never grew up in one particular place. We always boxed up to go to a new base assignment. I learned how to only take the essentials and set up a new household quickly."

"That is a skill, sweetheart," declared Raleigh proudly.

"No," replied Janice, shaking her head.

"I hate to break up this party," announced Heather to the group, "But it is way past my work day. Time for me to lock up."

On the way out the door Nancy overheard Raleigh stop Aen and offer to help get her banners ready in time for her performance. He suggested they get fabric markers. Why didn't Nancy think of that? It was an obvious solution. Raleigh could draw illustrations. When he said he would be more than delighted, Nancy knew he wasn't just being polite.

CHAPTER 13

A couple days later Janice dropped by the quilt store alone. Nancy realized that it was the first time she had seen her without Ann. Janice noticed the puzzled expression on her face.

"Oh, hi Nancy. Ann and I both wanted to come by, but she's home with the flu. I'm going to stop by Marconi's to get her take-out green chile chicken stew. They put in a bunch of different vegetables, plus they servedelicious warm bread sticks on the side."

The stew sounded strangely appealing to Nancy. She might grab a cup later in the afternoon.

"You know," said Janice, "green chile has lots of vitamin C."

She walked to the work table to lay out the quilt pieces she and Ann finished so far. Nancy was impressed by the progress they made in a couple days' time. She showed Janice how to run a basting stitch to use for the next step of the project. As Janice practiced with needle, thread, and fabric scraps, Nancy turned her attention to the store's sewing notions, which seemed to continually be a jumbled mess.

"Why don't you let me fix that?"

Nancy glanced up in surprise and watched Janice behind her survey the mess.

"I've never been any good at home organization or decorating," admitted Nancy. The sad plastic cupid in her front window almost seemed to nod in agreement.

"Oh, this is nothing. You should see my children's bedrooms. Being a mom really teaches you about dealing with messes."

Janice suddenly appeared awkward. "Oh, no. I'm sorry. I hope I didn't say anything to offend you. I mean, you don't have kids, right?"

Nancy got the distinct impression that Janice might slide away like a timid mouse running for cover. While her mood had improved since the other day, she was still unsure of herself. She seemed constantly worried about whether she said or did the wrong thing.

"Oh, that's fine," said Nancy, in her best reassuring voice. "I had a full life."

Janice couldn't help herself and asked, "Even without your own children? I can't imagine life without my husband or kids. They mean the entire world to me." She added, "I know we talked about this before, but being a wife and mother is everything I ever wanted."

"Don't you think about other things you could do?"

"Once in a while I have a bad day and think my life should be different. Honestly, the only part I regret is that we didn't have more children. Mike and I tried after the older ones went to school but it wasn't meant to be. I don't know why God choose for me to only have two. But I learned to trust His wisdom. I wasn't meant to raise little ones at home right now."

"Did you ever think about fostering or adoption?"

"Yes, but it never worked out. I learned to trust that I'm doing what God intended for me to do."

"I can understand it not working out," said Nancy. "I assumed when I was younger, after my divorce, that I would meet a nice guy and we'd start a family. But that never worked out, either."

"Don't you believe in love?"

Nancy stopped. What did she believe at this point? If she shared Janice's view God made a plan, then He certainly was a joker. Still, did she completely give up on the whole idea? "I suppose there is the rare possibility I could find love."

"If you want, I own really great books about loving that you can borrow."

"You need to read books on love?" asked a surprised Nancy.

"Yeah," Janice answered. "You know, even though my kids can frustrate me, I never have trouble loving them. However, being married to a man is kind of harder."

They both laughed.

"It's a challenge," she added. "I believe God intends for us to live in pairs, like Adam and Eve. Still, there are days that I forget. Sometimes it helps to get advice. I went to great workshops at my church. One workbook I'm reading right now talks about how love is a verb."

"Verb?"

"Right. It's a process. Too often we treat it like it's only a noun, like it somehow exists by itself. Love is action. We make love happen with our activities."

"How do you process love?"

Janice laughed again. "It's not about engaging in a process. It's not about going out and thinking that you'll find the already-perfect mate. He doesn't exist. It's about engaging in 'active love' by becoming the kind of person with the capacity to create love."

"Excuse me?"

"We spend all of our time thinking about what the other person will or won't do for us, when we really should spend our time figuring out how good we are at giving love. Do we do an adequate job of being a person with the capacity to build love?"

Nancy mulled the words over. She admitted, if only to herself, that she tended to judge her lovers harshly without spending much time examining herself. Was she a loving enough partner?

Nancy began to think back through her relationships to try to remember if she bothered to make any real efforts at a long-term commitment. Was that what she wanted now? Why did she equate "real love" with a long-term partnership? Maybe the occasional friend with bennies was fine.

In the past, she never put too much thought into what she really wanted. She tended to go along for the ride and see how things turned out on their own. It was more honest, right? Not try to manipulate a partner into pretending that he wanted to stay?

Truth to be told, after her divorce, she never gave commitment a good shot. Friends would point out she tended to pick men who were somehow not quite available—newly divorced, not ready for a relationship, or some who never gave anyone commitment.

She didn't need to think about her own ability to love if her partners weren't really available anyway. Was she capable of love? She remained lost in thought until she heard something hit the floor. She glanced over to see Janice pull apart her displays and rearrange them. She would offer a hand, but it was clear she would only get in the way. Janice was amazingly fast.

Soon her notions became beautifully organized in a new arrangement of containers.

"You're a miracle worker," said Nancy.

"Oh, it's nothing."

"No, Raleigh and Ann were right. You have a natural gift."

Janice blushed and said thanks. She seemed more at ease with herself while she created order out of chaos, and everything was neatly stacked in its rightful place. "If you don't mind me asking—do you know a special guy?"

Nancy shook her head no.

"I met someone recently, but he's the reason Fay and I have, umm, not been so close lately."

"She doesn't like your new beau?"

"No. Actually, we both like him."

"So she's jealous you're going out?"

"Oh, neither one of us dated him." Nancy paused. "Well, I guess I don't know. Maybe by now they have. He seemed to like her better."

The thought depressed her.

Janice said, "I heard Raleigh say something to Aen in class, which made me think neither one of you has someone special in your lives."

"Really?"

"Well, he didn't use such nice language, so I won't repeat his exact words."

Bless Raleigh.

"You know," said Nancy, "I'll think about what you told me today. You gave me a new perspective."

"It must be interesting to own a store and talk with so many different people."

"Oh, if only! I wish I made conversation with a lot of customers," said Nancy. She couldn't hide her sad expression.

"You look troubled. Do you want to talk about it? I'm a really good listener."

"Oh, I don't know."

Janice pulled out a couple chairs from the work table and they both sat down. Janice smiled patiently without pressuring Nancy to say anything. Usually her mind wandered, but Nancy found Janice's smile helped organize her thoughts as well.

"Sometimes," said Janice, "I find it helps to make lists. Okay, Ann tells me I go a little crazy with them, but they keep me really in shape. My lists help me solve problems. Sometimes you need to see everything, pro and con, written out on paper."

She casually reached over to the quilt binding bin to arrange the packages in neat rows as they talked. She continued, "For example, Mike and I started to think about where we'll retire when he leaves the service. We started to list the pros and cons of different places we could live."

"I did," said Nancy, "before I moved out west."

"What did you like best about Albuquerque?"

"Okay, I wasn't actually very thorough. I kind of thought of some places in general I might live. Maybe I didn't actually think through all the points. I never visited some cities I considered, like Denver."

"What were the pros about Denver?"

"I don't know. Let's see—there's more people? Which means I would attract a lot more shoppers to my store?"

"Okay, now think about the cons. Wouldn't a bigger city mean you have a lot more competition? Ann and I were in Colorado Springs recently and we noticed several quilt-related stores in the area. With all the good things come some bad things. The lists help you think through all the positives and negatives."

"Have you ever made a list about whether to close a store?"

Janice's head jerked up in surprise. She searched Nancy's face. "You're not serious, are you? You're such a fabulous teacher! Ann and I thought we would never learn how to make those patterns. You taught us how."

"Yeah, thanks, but the classes still aren't enough to keep paying my bills. If I stay open, in the next few months I'll need to spend down my retirement savings early. I already blew my parents' inheritance. At what point do I stop feeding the quilt shop, and keeping it on life support? Maybe this was a just a failure."

"Have you talked with Ann? She mentioned working with some clients in the same situation as you. She has some ideas about financial solutions to problems like yours."

"I didn't think of asking Ann. Short-term money still doesn't solve the overall problem of not enough sales, though."

"Didn't you tell us in class you started a website and doing all the stuff the kids do—like posting to, what's it called, Friend Book?"

"Facebook? Yeah, I started to work hard on it, but somehow got distracted."

"Maybe you need to make yourself a schedule. Even though I'm a housewife, if I don't make a daily plan I would never get anything done. People seem to think they can barge in on me because I don't have a real job. They can use my time however because I don't deal with a boss. You must get really strict. When do you work on your website?"

"Umm, when I'm not doing something else?"

"And when is that, usually?"

"Oh, yeah. Lately something else was always going on. I guess I figured I would do my marketing work whenever I thought of it."

"Ah, ha!" said Janice. "My kids used to have the same problem, which is why they used to have so much trouble getting homework done. I finally taught them to schedule their time effectively."

Nancy didn't like hearing she performed worse than Janice's high schoolers, although she admitted once again Janice possessed real organizing talent.

"Where did you learn all of this?"

"People think it's easy to be a housewife, but it's not if you do a good job. I learned from running my family. You must get very sharp at time and resource management. We live on one income."

Nancy found extra paper and they sat down to map out a new plan for the store. Janice encouraged her to keep a small notebook at all times so she could refine her lists of ideas, say, while she stood in line at the grocery store.

Strange, but Nancy saw instant results. In all her worries about her problems she neglected to send out her weekly email newsletter for a while. She wrote one and got a response the same day as a large surprise order from friends back home. Big enough, in fact, to cover more than the month's expenses. It would be her first month in the black.

All at once, she felt gratitude. She realized she was lucky to meet many special people in New Mexico. She could turn a profit despite the harsh economy. Perhaps a special magic lived on Gold Street.

Nancy realized in that moment she wouldn't close the quilt shop. Janice helped her create a plan to make the store work.

If only Nancy could try her advice on love. Would she always be alone?

CHAPTER 14

Nancy's quilting store was back on track, but her friendship with Fay was not. It was strange to not stop next door for freshly brewed tea. Nancy decided to make the best of it and get hot chai at the Jumping Bean Café across the street.

Stella was sitting with her niece when Nancy came through the door.

"So I hear you finally had enough of Fay," said Stella dramatically.

It was much too early in the day to deal with Stella. She tried to ignore the situation and proceeded to place her order.

"Well, so you know," remarked Stella with a flourish of her hands and the sweep of her dress, "you still have friends on Gold Street."

Stella did not commit herself as one of those friends. Nancy decided it was just as well.

Nancy put some space between Stella and herself. Despite their falling out, she still felt loyal to Fay and missed their friendship. Nancy turned her back on Stella and picked up her order from the counter.

As Nancy brought the steaming hot liquid to her mouth, Stella called out, "I don't even believe those rumors about you dating Mary Ann's husband."

Nancy choked and gulped at the same time. Hot chai burned her throat at the same moment it prevented her from breathing. She swallowed and gasped for air. Theresa M ran from behind the counter and hit her on the back to help her breathe again.

Stella merely sauntered out the door.

When Nancy could fully breathe again she turned to Theresa M with wide eyes. The café owner shrugged her shoulders and said, "You'll have to excuse my Tia Stella. She's just like that."

"A witch?" inquired Nancy.

"No," replied Theresa M, "just dramatic."

Nancy sat down to nurse her remaining chai. Theresa M busied herself with wiping the counters until she couldn't stand it any longer.

"So is it true?"

Nancy looked horrified.

"I only ask because he did the same thing to Tia Stella. He left her a note asking to meet him at some lame restaurant at Cottonwood Mall. He said he would bring her half a dozen roses. Turns out he gave the other half to his wife. We saw Mary Ann with them the next day."

Nancy closed her eyes and sighed. She wasn't about to tell anyone she only merited a single rose.

"He didn't use the Alibi newspaper to ask your Aunt Stella out?"

It was Theresa M's turn for wide eyes. "That was your blind date? From the 'I Saw You' ad?" She started to connect the pieces of Nancy's blind date story together in her mind. "I helped you answer the ad to go out with Mary Ann's husband? Oh, no."

"Oh, yes."

Theresa M continued to wipe the counters in silence.

"Wait a minute," said Nancy. "Does Mary Ann know about me? I mean, I didn't actually eat dinner with her husband at the restaurant, but I accidently showed up."

The younger woman contemplated the situation. "I'm not sure she knows it was you. Tia Stella ate lunch at Marconi's the other day and saw Mary Ann totally freak out as she talked to Mrs. Marconi. Tia heard her husband was seen coming on to another woman. Tia worried it was about her, but then she realized it sounded more like someone else. The description fits you."

"Me?"

"Yeah, Mary Ann heard the rumor it was some plain older lady with a short haircut, baggy pants and a frumpy sweater. Tia knew that definitely wasn't her."

Nancy tried to hide the hurt look on her face. Theresa M looked apologetic.

"Okay," said Nancy with a stiff upper lip, "that's still not enough for Mary Ann to figure out it was me."

"Maybe," said Theresa M, but she didn't sound convinced.

Nancy looked around the coffee shop distractedly. She looked through the display counter and noticed for the first time the young café owner was busy texting with her left hand.

"You're texting someone while talking with me?" asked Nancy in annoyance.

"You don't want me to talk with Keisha?" asked a perplexed Theresa M. "Keisha says hi and wants to know if we're all still going to the plant expo this weekend?"

Nancy had no clue how the two young women could communicate such long conversations when limited to 140 characters a message. "Umm, yeah," she replied, but she still debated about the expo. Did she really want to see Dr. Bob chat happily with Fay? How could she compete with the elegant woman? Did Dr. Bob see a woman lost in frumpy sweaters when he compared Nancy and Fay side by side? She never considered what she must look like standing next to Fay before.

"And Keisha says you're a beautiful person. On the inside."

"Thanks… I think."

Nancy nursed her chai as she watched the front door of her store. It was shaping up to be another slow winter day.

She would somehow get through another lonely Valentine's Day. The plant expo might actually cheer her up. Looking at garden displays and ignoring the attendees, anyway. Next week's quilting class would run more smoothly. Luckily, V-Day would be over by then. It was time to think about the coming spring as a season of change, blooming, and all that.

She wondered if it was time to get seeds. She didn't think about it all winter. Right after she bought her house, her next door neighbor suggested she join the neighborhood seedling swap. It suddenly dawned on her; warm weather would come much earlier to Albuquerque than her old town in Indiana. It was time to think new things instead of sit in her shop all day full of worry.

She didn't know about the growing seasons here. She never mastered much planting back home either. Her little hobby farm, back in Indiana, was more of a holding pen for rescue cats and dogs than agriculture. She was a sucker for hurt and abandoned pets. She never got around to crops, or even a few tomatoes. Wouldn't it be ironic if she found her green thumb while living downtown in a city?

Planning her landscape would also give her an excuse to talk with Dr. Bob, but about xeric gardening, of course.

Theresa M came from around the counter to sit with Nancy at the table. She looked indecisive, like she wanted to say something, but didn't know how to go about it.

"Spit it out."

"Well, umm. Say, why don't we visit Keisha at the mall Saturday night?"

"You two young ladies want to walk around a mall with me?"

"No," answered Theresa M, a little too firmly. She softened. "Keisha got a new job at the place where everyone walks around outdoors, even when it's raining, too hot or very cold."

"You mean ABQ Uptown?"

Nancy heard about the lifestyle mall. Fay told her she waited years for better women's clothing shops and fancier stores like Pottery Barn or Williams-Sonoma. However, Fay still did the majority of her shopping while visiting friends in places like Scottsdale or Miami.

Nancy, on the other hand, made her last shopping trip at Sears. She knew Sears didn't bode well for her personal style, but the store advertised a two-for-one coupon on holiday sweaters with little bells and ribbons sewed on. She adored any tops with reindeer or happy elves; although even she admitted the sweater featuring Santa's back end was a horrible mistake.

Nancy turned to Theresa M, "I need help, don't I?"

"Can I be totally honest? Like, totally?"

Nancy mulled it over and replied truthfully, "No. Do not be honest. Be polite." She knew she was not ready for the brutal truth from the mouth of babes.

"Yeah, okay," said Theresa M, but she seemed at a loss for words. She suddenly brightened. "Keisha just got a job at one of those mature ladies clothing shops."

"Okay."

"They are thinking of maybe making her a personal shopper. You know, to help you pick out your outfits. The store never hired one before, but they think Keisha is doing such a good job of helping women find stuff she could get a promotion and higher commissions. The customers are really happy and would never think of how to put together new looks without her advice."

"That's great for Keisha."

"You could be her first official customer."

"Oh, no."

The two women began to argue, albeit in a friendly manner. Nancy could not see the point of spending so much money on something as frivolous as nicer clothing.

Theresa M countered Nancy didn't teach anymore. She was now a retail store owner and needed to project a successful image. She was the face of her business. She sold herself as much as her quilting supplies. Did she want people to think quilting was frumpy?

Nancy conceded they were good points, even if the last one hurt.

In truth, she also thought about her love life. How would she ever meet a special man? Did anyone post ads reading—*Wanted: Gal Who Knows How to Fill a Reindeer Sweater. Frumpy Preferred.*

Nancy looked over and realized the young woman hid one hand under the table.

"You're texting Keisha again!"

That explained the persuasive arguments. Keisha must be using her new sales training. Was she trying to sucker Nancy into buying new clothes?

"I don't know about this."

"So it's all set up," replied Theresa M, ignoring the last comment. "We're going to meet Keisha at her store after you close the quilt shop on Saturday. We can go for the evening. The manager will leave Keisha the keys. We can stay as late as we want."

"How much does Keisha think she is going to sell?"

Theresa M still ignored her comments. "She gave you homework. You need to bring at least five magazine photos or computer print-outs of outfits you like. Oh, and we need to bring appetizers and champagne. We're going to make it a fun girls' night out." The younger woman looked up and smiled. "I'll bring the food if you can handle the booze. I don't know anything about bubbly stuff anyway."

Nancy decided it would be educational for everyone.

****

Nancy found herself pacing the rest of the week. Her inner frugal demon tortured her. How could she spend too much money on clothes?

At home, standing in front of her mirror, she felt worse. How could she not update her look? Could her current wardrobe even be termed style? When exactly did she start to look so old? She saw her mother reflected in the mirror. It wasn't just the way her butt rearranged itself to the front of her stomach, or the number of laugh lines she accumulated on her face. She must be very amusing indeed.

No, she realized, it was the fact she looked like all her old married friends, as if she stopped trying to look better many years earlier. She gave up the fight. She let herself go.

Nancy finally conceded to herself she was lucky to befriend two young women willing to help her get out of her rut. She would probably disagree with whatever odd outfits they concocted for her, but they would help her banish her old sweaters for good.

Looking hard into the mirror, she decided it was time to invest in herself. She was truly ready to do it. It was time to take her life fully into her own hands.

She felt sadness, though, for not discussing her plans with Fay. She decided she would work on reconciliation with Fay as well. She could become the better person and break the ice.

Nancy went online and began to read dating advice. Of course, many of the articles were written to market a product or service. Even so, she read over and over about the need to meet a lot of men. Chasing after one guy was desperate. She swallowed hard. That hit too close to home. She resolved it was time to look into more options, starting with a pile of dating and advice books from the library, and figuring out which dating service to join, because she would never meet enough men in the quilt shop, that was for sure.

One dating expert suggested she should spend twenty percent of her annual income on finding a husband. Ouch. These folks obviously did not own retail stores, nor did the experts who suggested she should spend untold hours taking up multiple hobbies and joining various clubs. She worked six full days a week in her store, then spent the seventh fixing her old house, as well as summer gardening.

On her schedule, she needed speed dating. Every other option seemed too time-consuming.

CHAPTER 15

Nancy arrived at ABQ Uptown with a bottle of local sparkling wine called Gruet. She chose the light bodied Demi Sec for its dessert quality. The evening for the three women began in the break room, where Nancy explained the difference between true Champagne, produced in a specific region in France, and everything else labeled as sparkling wine. They left the bottle to chill in the employee fridge as they headed to the sales floor. Drinking would come after the rest of the customers left.

Nancy couldn't imagine what they could do to fill so much time. Usually she never spent more than half an hour in the women's department. She began to glance nervously at racks of clothes while Keisha examined her in great detail. Keisha named Theresa M official assistant, tasked with finding colors and correct sizes.

"Do we start with tops or bottoms?" asked Nancy.

"Neither," answered Keisha. "I will show you Spanx. If you want to look good each and every day, you will put it on."

"Tia Stella always wears Spanx," said Theresa M.

"Maybe that explains her bad moods," said Nancy.

Nancy wasn't sure exactly what Spanx was, but knew from the sound of the name she wouldn't enjoy it. Despite her impromptu lecture about women's liberation, bra burning, and the failed Equal Rights Amendment, they both still insisted she should wear it. Daily.

Nancy begrudgingly tried on Spanx undergarments. She allowed she would consider it on special occasions, such as her own funeral.

Keisha began to realize they were in for an even longer night than she planned.

Next item of business was fitting Nancy for new bras. She never gave them much thought, but Keisha discovered she was wearing the wrong size. The bands were too small and the cup size too big. The young woman explained ill-fitting bras were a common problem. No wonder Nancy was a bit saggy and always covered up with over-sized tops and bulky sweaters.

Keisha rooted through their inventory to and found bras with as much structural engineering as a bridge. Luckily they also engineered padding in the straps.

Nancy admitted while the new bras felt constricting at first, she also stood up straighter and displayed a better frame. While nature seemed intent to let gravity soften her into a squishy ball, Keisha helped her regain a shapelier feminine silhouette.

She looked down at her watch and realized an entire hour went by and they still worked on underwear. The young women brought sexy and fun panties to the dressing room. Nancy made them leave the dressing stall. She wasn't about to let them see her full birthday suit, and handed back the thongs without trying them on. She successfully retained some dignity. Still, they scouted out great finds she never would try on by herself.

While Nancy did talk herself into a clothing budget, she debated about spending so much money on undergarments nobody would ever see. All this would cost a small fortune and she hadn't reached the main event. She remembered her resolve to start dating. She found herself talking about wanting a special man to the young women. Keisha and Theresa M dashed off, and returned with even racier underwear.

They gave Nancy a lecture about why dressing more provocatively did not transform anyone into a slut; the whole reason for women's liberation was to wear whatever one wanted; not to cover up like a sack of potatoes! The idea of good girls and bad girls went out of date along with deep shag carpeting.

Nancy needed to get with the twenty-first century, embrace the feminine woman she was, and should never, ever, under any circumstances, wear another pair of mom jeans. They picked up a store catalogue and forced her to swear on it.

"So you want my crack to show every time I bend over?" asked Nancy.

They were now well into the bottle of Gruet, and would send Theresa M out for another. The appetizers of tortilla roll-ups with cream cheese, olives and green chile were delicious.

"Okay, that's really a problem," admitted Keisha. "Too many clothes are designed to fit young skinny bodies. It's hard to find anything flattering which doesn't compete with teenagers and looks good on a full-figured woman. The clothes here were designed to work on a mature body."

"My friends always complain about their moms shopping at the same stores as them," said Theresa M. "But my mom doesn't want to go anywhere. She wears the same stuff as twenty years ago—like you, Nancy. No offense. It's not cool vintage stuff, either."

"It's too depressing to go shopping at my age," said Nancy, as she felt the wine go to her head.

Okay," said Keisha, taking command of the situation. "We're going to find you a great style. If you see pictures of movie stars like Diane Keaton, whom my mom loves, she looks fabulous even though she's old."

"Diane Keaton is not old," argued Nancy.

"Buying her birthday candles would cost a lot more than the cake," said Theresa M.

"Look," interjected Keisha, "we have a job to do tonight. Did you bring some pictures of outfits you like?"

The three women looked over the selection of photos. Keisha used her talented eye. She was like a hair dresser: able to explain how a cut might look good on a model in a magazine, but won't work for every hair type or texture. Some styles would complement Nancy's figure better than others.

Once Keisha got a sense of the clothing Nancy found appealing, she took out their store catalogue again to show her some possible combinations.

Keisha proceeded to give her basic lessons about dressing Nancy never considered before. From the interested look on Theresa M's face, she realized style was acquired through practice and guidance. Fay probably could give her some tips, but Nancy never bothered to ask.

Keisha started her lesson, and explained the easiest way to look pulled together was to coordinate types of fabric, shades of color, and general style of clothing. For example, a shiny polyester blend shirt might stay wrinkle free while traveling, but might not look right paired with a casual linen jacket and a cotton skirt.

The fiber content, weight, and so on should all be considered when pulling together an outfit.

There were exceptions to the rules for women with advanced knowledge of dress. The previously mentioned example might work if all of the garments were shades of beige and looked like they were paired intentionally, but Keisha advised Nancy to stick to the basics to start.

The next lesson was how to look polished by coordinating any metals worn together. Nancy never gave thought about whether silver buttons on a jacket might clash with her gold necklace, or thought she should wear several pairs of reading glasses to go with different outfits. Keisha even encouraged them to think about the metal clasps on their shoes and purses. Nancy didn't admit she carried one purse for the last three years, through all seasons, regardless of her clothing.

Keisha said even the metal on their zippers counted.

Nancy suddenly realized this would be way harder than she imagined. She dismissed style as a hobby for the rich or very bored. It began to dawn on her creating her own look would take actual work, like picking out the right fabric for an intricate quilt design. She needed to stop throwing on the first clothes she reached in her closet in the morning.

Keisha told Nancy to try on basic dresses, skirts, and pants to get a sense of what suited her body type the best. At that point,

Nancy began to panic. How many items of clothing would she need to buy?

Keisha patiently explained the next lesson. The key was a few well-made staples to base her entire wardrobe around. She should invest in work horses and could add only one or two new basics each season.

She would spice up her wardrobe with great accessories. The key was to invest in clothes that fit exactly right and flatter her figure. She could do more with a few correct basics than an entire closet full of cheap, ill-fitted garments. Only young women could get away with flimsy, cheap and trendy outfits.

"Have you seen the Six Items or Less challenges on the internet?" asked Keisha.

Nancy shook her head no.

"It was way cool," said Theresa M. "We did it last year. We logged on to a website and posted six things we would wear for an entire 30 days."

"Underwear, socks, tights and accessories didn't count," added Keisha. "It was fabulous. It totally made me rethink my wardrobe. Like, who thought you could wear so few things? It really got me in touch with what is important. That's what got me started on helping other people rethink their clothes."

"Yeah," said Theresa M, "I was lost. I didn't know what to wear. Keisha helped me put together this hot mod look using what I already own and cool vintage stuff we found at thrift stores."

"How come we're not at a vintage store right now?" asked Nancy.

"Well, umm, it's harder to find larger sizes and it takes a really long time," Keisha tried to explain tactfully. "Plus, Theresa M won't keep those clothes for long. They're too trendy. She's going to trade them out each season. It's cheap, fun stuff. We're building a long-term wardrobe for you with high quality clothes to last a few years. Mature women can look really old in outdated clothing."

"Yeah," said Theresa M. "I already got rid of the outfits we found last year. I'm tired of 1960s London already. This year I'm going multi-cultural. Aen, from your quilting class, stopped into the café the other day. She's way cool and I totally dig her style. I see her around with slam poets. I'm going to do something like that. La Raza Unida. I will get in touch with my Mesoamerican roots."

"You're going to use Aen as a role model?" asked a worried Nancy.

"So anyway," said Keisha, bringing the other women back to the present, "the idea is to get your closet down to the most fundamental pieces. Consider it basic, like the cake. You can change the decoration with trendier items."

The other customers had long since left by the time the three women found Nancy her wardrobe staples. They started with black, but they all agreed the color was too harsh. It might look okay for a corporate job in a northern city, but it was too formal for Albuquerque. It also seemed to wash out her coloring.

Pastels, on the other hand, weren't quite right either. Nancy felt like an Easter egg. If they lived in the Florida Keys or Santa Monica, the colors might seem okay.

Keisha held more colors against Nancy's skin. Theresa M noticed a lighter shade of navy blue seemed to work best with her skin tone and hair.

Nancy would never believe the process could be so arduous, but she now found the base color for her new wardrobe. She mentally began to go through dozens of items she could get rid of because they were bad colors for her.

Keisha proceeded to instruct them about various shades of white to pair with the navy. She held a white jacket to Nancy's skin, but it seemed to bleach her out as much as the black. She showed the others how white comes in many undertones, only some of which are complimentary.

"Keep that in mind for your wedding dresses," said Keisha.

The other two women merely rolled their eyes. Despite their differences in age, neither seemed inclined to wear a white gown or take a trip down the aisle.

Keisha picked one of the whites and held it against her own mocha skin. While terrible for Nancy, it was quite becoming her. She repeated the experiment with Theresa M's olive complexion.

As they continued to look at colors and skin tones, Keisha suddenly got an idea. Nancy's hair would be charitably called honey ash mixed with increasing gray, although she referred to it as dishwater blond.

"Have you ever tried dying your hair red?" asked Keisha.

"So I'll look like Stella?" replied Nancy.

Theresa M scowled at the pair.

"No," said Keisha, "not flaming red. A much more subtle color. It should be done mixed with highlights, not a single color from a box at home. Boxed hair dye only seems to look good on girls in their twenties and early thirties. After that, it's time to go to a salon, for sure."

Keisha held the navy blue once again against Nancy's skin. "I'm sure that's the missing piece of the puzzle. You were meant for subtle red hair. I noticed redheads look best in the colors we chose for you. You'll be amazed."

Against Nancy's protests, the two young women texted their friends until they found a salon they trusted to take Nancy early Sunday before her quilt shop opened. She would be a new woman by the time they went to the plant expo in the evening.

The young fashion maven coaxed the older woman to try on more outfits until they arrived at some conclusions. First of all, most pants did not flatter Nancy. At the very least she should get them professionally altered to fit her short height. She mostly looked better in dresses or skirts.

Next, they decided she looked best with a covered waistline. She was at a point in life where she should wear shirts hanging out or wear a jacket or light sweater to cover her middle. Under no circumstances, no matter what the prevailing fashion trends, should she wear a belt or decorative scarf around her waist.

Keisha encouraged her to find alternative ways to create a waistline with some type of fitting, such as darts, or perhaps a jacket that stopped at her waistline. Tent dresses and other shapeless garments were as unflattering as a belt.

Everyone agreed mid-length dresses and skirts most complimented Nancy's figure. Right at the knee was ideal, but she might even get away with a slightly shorter length paired with opaque tights. She must be careful with long skirts. Many styles swallowed her short frame like a whale and mid-calf lengths gave her a matronly look.

Looking at her style transformation in the mirror, Nancy became excited.

She picked out a basic sheath dress in a navy blue. Keisha told her try to on a couple matching tailored jackets to show her they gave her a better shape than most sweaters. Nancy picked out a three-quarters sleeve jacket with fabric covered buttons. She didn't need to want to worry about matching metals. Next she found a dark gray skirt, and a pink champagne top she never would have consider buying by herself.

Keisha showed her how to mix and match the outfits. She could, for example, wear the pink top over or under the dress, add the jacket or not, or switch the pink top to the skirt.

She could then work with some of the clothes already in her closet, although Keisha challenged her to go through her existing wardrobe and shrink it to about a dozen garments. Six items if she was really up to the task.

"You're joking right?"

"How many clothes of better quality do you own?"

"That's not the point."

"Yes, it is," said Keisha. "It's like eating fast food. You binge on greasy hamburgers and salty fries every day, instead of a few basic quality ingredients. Get rid of the junk."

Nancy mentally went through her closet. The young fashion expert was correct. Her wardrobe reflected volume rather than well-chosen pieces of exceptional style or fit. Nothing was tailored to her unique body frame. She admitted a new truth to herself: becoming more stylish meant shopping and living in a more conscious manner. Done correctly, she would buy fewer clothes and make them last a lot longer. Keisha gave her the name of a seamstress who could do a few nips and tucks to make her clothes look custom.

"Won't I get bored with so few clothes?"

"No," replied both young women at once, "accessorize."

Accessorize was the young women's mantra when they took the challenge to wear only six items for a month. Keisha could tie a scarf a hundred different ways. Theresa M particularly enjoyed finding trinkets such as jewelry. She was forever rearranging the decorations in her café, inheriting her aunt's flair for the dramatic touch.

The older woman was worn out, but couldn't resist when the two younger women presented her with a pile of scarves, necklaces, bracelets and earrings. She watched in amazement as Keisha expertly wrapped cloth around her neck to demonstrate different techniques for tying knots in a scarf. Theresa M complimented the looks with perfect earrings, bracelets and necklaces.

Nancy realized Keisha was right. She could totally change the presentation of her basic clothes with her accessories. The right change of scarves and jewelry created a whole new outfit.

Keisha didn't recommend purchasing any of the cheap jewelry in her store. In a place like Albuquerque, handmade jewels were available at steep discounts, particularly silver. There was no reason to wear fake plastic except vintage jewelry at the flea market.

Keisha talked Nancy into buying a couple scarves. They practiced draping them again.

At the end of the shopping trip Nancy realized she didn't really spend much money. Yes, it was equal to her clothing budget for the last couple years, but since Keisha did such a good job of educating her on how to work with a few garments, Nancy wouldn't need much. She felt wonderful in better clothing.

She also knew a private image consultant would cost her beaucoup bucks. She received an excellent deal for the young woman's advice.

"You should open a clothing store on Gold Street," said Nancy. "I mean, once you build a client base and know what styles sell best."

"That would be totally awesome," seconded Theresa M. "I could help you find jewelry to sell."

"Yeah, that's cool," said Keisha, but didn't sound convinced she could do it. She tipped back the last of the second bottle of Gruet wine. "Hey, we didn't figure out what I'm going to do about my project and Cute Guy next door."

"Wait," said Theresa M, "we'll talk about it tomorrow evening at the plant expo. This is Nancy's night."

"Okay," said a disappointed Keisha.

Nancy felt guilty. She didn't think about Keisha's dilemma all evening because she was so focused on herself. She was now exhausted and still completely out of ideas. She promised herself she would concentrate on the Cute Guy problem tomorrow.

As the three women left the ABQ Uptown store, they made Nancy promise she would keep her hair appointment in the morning.

CHAPTER 16

Nancy was lost in thought rearranging fabric notions when police officers burst through her front door late Sunday morning. She was tired from her late night of shopping and early hair appointment. However, she found an unexpected reserve of energy to go with her new look.

She glanced up in surprise at the officers and noticed an embarrassed Rachel behind them. Her face turned several shades of bright red.

"Oh my God! I didn't know it was you," stammered Rachel.

"Is everything okay, ladies?" inquired one of the men in blue. Nancy noticed he wore a lot of stripes on his uniform and was rather attractive. Was he smiling at her?

"Of course it's me." She turned to the policemen. "I own this store."

She noticed the younger officer seemed to feel a soft spot for Rachel. "Is everything in order?" he asked Rachel.

"I am so sorry," said Rachel. "I didn't even recognize Nancy. You don't look like you! I thought someone broke into your store."

"Were quilting thieves around here lately?" asked the bemused older officer.

Nancy noticed his hazel eyes and deep smile. He was rather athletic for his maturity without an ounce of flab she could detect. She wondered if he still maintained a washboard stomach. She suddenly pictured herself touching his middle to find out. She gave him her best grin and thought to herself—what would Raleigh say? She would need to work on flirting, because she clearly wasn't ready for men whom unexpectedly turned up in her store.

"Everything is fine," is all she could muster.

The younger officer looked hesitantly at Rachel and muttered something about leaving if no further assistance was needed.

"There is a coffee shop across the street," said Rachel. "I mean, if you have time. My students won't be at the yoga studio for another twenty minutes. I feel so bad about calling you here for nothing."

"Beg your pardon," said the mature officer. "We just heard another call come in."

Neither woman paid attention to the background voices on the officer radios. As the two walked out, Nancy heard the younger one remark he might take up yoga classes.

"Forgive me," said Rachel to Nancy. "You aren't you. You look fabulous. Fifteen years younger easily. Did you lose weight? Oh, wait a minute. I just saw you two days ago. That's not possible. Look at your hair. You totally look like a natural redhead. Like, for real. That's what really confused me. The cut is awesome. Your clothes are different, too. Really stylish now."

Rachel seemed to go on and on.

Nancy and Rachel never spent much time together, so Nancy understood how her neighbor might make the mistake.

She was a new person.

She felt her best in ages. She day-dreamed about the coming plant expo. Afterward, she would go with Keisha and Theresa M to dinner and find an appropriate dating service. She was finally ready.

Nancy was engrossed at the plant expo. As her two young friends chatted with several friends, she read the labels of every seed packet and inspected every plant she could get her hands on. She was determined to start flowers for the yard.

She heard a familiar voice from behind.

"Have you seen Nancy yet?" asked Fay.

"She's over by the display of geraniums," said Jane.

Nancy whirled around. Fay gasped at the remarkable change in Nancy, although Jane didn't look surprised.

"How did you know that was Nancy?" demanded Fay. "I didn't recognize her at all."

Jane answered as if the woman in question wasn't standing in front of them. "She made some wonderful exterior improvements, but her aura isn't changed much."

"What?" asked a bewildered Nancy. She wasn't sure if she Jane insulted her or not.

Jane walked over to the quilt shop owner to explain. Fay hesitantly trailed behind her. "You look fabulous. However, the colors of your aura are still about the same, stronger even, because you are in a better state of mind. That's why I could recognize you from behind despite your external make-over. You merely got in touch with parts of yourself you hid behind baggy clothes while you pretended not to care. Your beauty was always inside of you. You simply let it out."

The rest of the women looked at Jane in stupefied silence. Theresa M and Keisha now listened.

"I know you don't believe me," Jane said, "but I can see a lot about each of you from your auras. For example, Theresa M—you and your young friend here don't possess fully developed auras. You need to be careful to protect yourselves. And," she added, "stop letting so many men into them."

The women stared at her in disbelief.

"I mean it," she lectured. "Every time you sleep with a man, he stays in your aura for seven years, even if it was just a one night stand. Think about that. And Theresa M, there are two men competing for too much of your energy. You are getting depleted."

She turned to the older women, "You two don't seem to have that problem. If anything, your auras are rather blank."

They looked back at Jane rather crossly.

"Jane, dear," said an annoyed Fay, "you know we love you. Really, but sometimes you are so California."

The two younger women looked even more uncomfortable as they watched their sex lives discussed in public by a trio of mature women. They made their excuses, and then dashed off to find more friends.

The three remaining women were left in awkward silence. They started to drift among the displays of plants.

"You do look absolutely wonderful," said Fay to Nancy.

"Keisha has an amazing eye for clothes," answered Nancy. "She was the friend of Theresa M's you just met tonight. She's also a student in my class."

She proceeded to tell the other two about the previous night and how the younger women figured out a new style and hair color. Nancy was proud of her new fashion sense and noted Fay's silver zipper and buttons clashed with her gold necklace, although she didn't mention it out loud.

Fay and Jane both vowed to go to the store where Keisha worked to update of their own wardrobes. The store manager would be crazy not to give her the personal shopper position.

As the three women continued among the plants, Fay and Nancy's friendship began to blossom again under Jane's watchful eye. Jane seemed able to create friendly energy wherever she went.

Before they realized what happened, they found themselves in front of Dr. Bob's xeriscape display.

"Well, hello ladies!" called out Bob. He looked delighted to see them. "I'm so glad you could make it. I was beginning to wonder. Who is your special friend?" He chattered on and on, clearly glad to be in the limelight. "Oh, see, I finally found old tablecloths to use for our display. My daughter assures me they are a vintage floral. Nothing washes like pure plastic. I'm sure it's not as good as something from Nancy's store. I kind of ran out of time and found them in the garage."

The women stared with open mouths.

Dr. Bob came out from behind the table and walked towards them with arms outstretched; he was ready for a deep embrace.

"Say," said Nancy, backing away, glancing at her watch, "I should get to the poppy table. They are ready to sell out. I read I must use drought resistant flowers for my yard. I'm thinking lots of red." She started to dash off.

"Hey wait," called Fay, "Do you think poppies could work in my yard? I mean, if I decided not to water an area of my lawn? I need to talk with them before their garden expert leaves."

Fay and Jane hooked arms, and made a beeline after Nancy.

Dr. Bob stopped mid-stride and his arms dropped to his side. He looked rather perplexed as he watched the three women disappear into the crowd.

****

Nancy met Keisha and Theresa M as planned for dinner. Fay and Jane decided to join them. They crowded around a table at Garcia's Kitchen, near Old Town on Route 66. As the women pursued the menu of New Mexican food, the subject of Keisha's quilt project finally came up.

Keisha filled everyone in on all the details as the women dipped their fresh warm tortilla chips into a bowl of tangy salsa, and mulled over the situation.

"Oh, dear," said Fay. "I can't think of any social etiquette I ever heard to deal with a situation like this. After all, you did not intentionally steal the young man's clothes. You honestly thought the bag was intended for donation."

"Why not go ahead and use them?" asked Theresa M. "After all, they are already cut to pieces. You can't give them back now."

"But it still doesn't seem right," said Nancy. "It's one thing to take them innocently, but it's another to go ahead and use them knowing they really belong to Cute Guy's brother."

"That's an excellent point," said Jane. "Keisha meant to tap into the psychic energy of Cute Guy, right?"

"Umm, I guess," replied Keisha. However, she didn't look convinced.

"Well," said Jane, "instead of connecting with Cute Guy, you'll pick up his brother's energy instead. This isn't at all what you intended."

"Would he believe the cat shredded the clothing if you put it back in the hallway? Got any feral cats?" asked Theresa M.

Fay said sternly, "Why not tell the truth and explain the mistake honestly?"

Keisha mulled the tactic over in her mind.

The group continued to discuss the pros and cons as the main entrees of enchiladas and burritos arrived. Nancy asked for an extra side of green chile. They split a pitcher of margaritas.

As dinner progressed it became obvious Keisha never found any easy answers. The group didn't come up with a quick and painless fix. She could throw away the bag and pretend it never happened. Except, as Jane pointed out, it would forever be on her conscious. Jane went so far as to declare it would create a black energy in the hallway, preventing her from meeting Cute Guy, although Keisha didn't look convinced about energies, black or otherwise.

After her second full drink, Fay blurted out, "You know our store magic doesn't work when used for the wrong purposes. Keisha needs to do her quilt fabric project with an open and loving heart to help someone else. That's what we do on Gold Street."

The table fell silent.

Keisha and Nancy glanced around the others in surprise. What an unusual thing for Fay to say, except everyone else appeared sheepish, not taken aback, as if a secret was revealed.

Did they drink too much? The single pitcher of margaritas was much stronger than Nancy imagined. She and Keisha stared at each other in wonder. Obviously they were the two people at the table who didn't know what was going on.

"Hey," said Nancy to the group, trying to make light of the situation, "you have to let us in on the joke. Because you're telling us an inside joke about magic on Gold Street, right?"

They looked to the other faces for an answer. Soon everyone turned to Jane to provide some sort of guidance.

"Yes, well," started Jane slowly. She fiddled with her napkin as she searched for her next words. "As Fay said, we should do loving things with an open heart." She cleared her throat.

"I'm still on the part about the magical stores," said Keisha. She clearly would not let the subject drop. She turned to stare Theresa M directly in the eyes.

"Okay, if you want an answer, I'll give you one," said Theresa M, but she was interrupted by a chorus of "No!" from Fay and Jane.

"Wow, these drinks are strong," said Nancy, willing the women to talk about normal things, like regular people eating dinner in a restaurant. Jane and her auras and energies became too weird sometimes, but why did Fay say such an odd thing? It wasn't like her at all.

"You're right dear," said Fay. "I think these drinks went straight to my head and now I'm talking nonsense. Good thing you'll drive me home Jane."

"Good thing indeed," said Jane. The two women gave Theresa M scowls.

"Okay, you win," said Theresa M, as she crossed her arms across her chest. "Give us alcohol and the next thing you know, we make jokes about Gold Street."

Later in the dinner Nancy observed Theresa M's and Keisha's hands below the big wooden table. She was certain they continued the bizarre conversation through text.

Did Nancy want to ask Fay more? If there really was a big secret, did she want to hear about their deluded beliefs?

What if she learned these women were all part of some weirdo cult? Or something more benign, like the time one of her colleagues invited her to a career networking party which turned out to be an Amway presentation on multi-level marketing? A little voice in the back of her head told her some things are better left unknown.

After all, none of the magic mumbo-jumbo involved her quilt shop, right?

Nancy was lost trying to escape her own thoughts when Keisha announced her decision about her quilt project. She would do the right thing, and do it with a loving heart; she would tell the truth to Cute Guy about what happened to his brother's clothes and offer to replace them. She would own up to her mistake.

The group congratulated her on her courage. Jane added some strange remark about the Spirit of Life being with Keisha.

Nancy decided she needed to put more space between Jane and herself. Granted, Jane was the one to talk Fay into attending the plant expo and mending their friendship. At the same time, if there was such a thing as weird energy, Jane was gifted in spades.

CHAPTER 17

Valentine's Day found Nancy seated in the tea shop. It felt like she had been gone a long time from Fay's life. She cradled a steaming brew in her hands and decided she would ignore the idiotic subject of magic on Gold Street. Women her age should be more careful about how much they drink with New Mexican food.

Fay complimented her on her outfit. Nancy still dressed sharp.

Nancy brought a flower seed catalogue. The two women poured over the pictures.

"I'm really serious about this," said Nancy. "I spent the last couple weeks researching growing flowers in the Southwest while I was up half the night." She didn't add her insomnia occurred after her big fight with Fay. Since they reunited at the plant expo, she slept like a baby at night.

Fay thumbed through the pages. "I don't enjoy the idea of tearing out my lawn, but I could add something around the border to perk it up."

"Maybe we could find you some flowers to go with the irrigation you already use on your grass, then you wouldn't need to increase your water use."

They were so engrossed with the pictures that they didn't hear the front door open.

"Why, you're both here!" exclaimed Dr. Bob. He held two tulips, one in each hand.

"Nice to see you," said Fay, but she didn't bother to get up.

He gave both women a huge smile. "Look, I brought one for each of you." He thrust his hands forward.

Nancy wondered what happened to the rest of the dozen. Did tulips come in dozens?

"Lovely," said Fay. Turning to Nancy, "Do you want both flowers? You could use them to perk up the sad little cupid in your window."

Nancy laughed heartily. "Good thought, but I don't have own vases. You should take them both. You're the one with all the decorative containers."

The flowers dropped to Dr. Bob's side. He looked at the two women the way a puppy stares longingly through a window, tail wagging, waiting to be let inside.

"Um, ladies, do you have plans for tonight?" he asked hopefully.

"I'm trying to decide," said Nancy.

"Really?" asked Fay brightly. "You already got replies from the new dating service?"

"I can't believe I let those two young women talk me into signing up Sunday night after dinner. We went with the mature singles service. Seems rather dignified, and I did get a couple offers today to go out tonight. Guess everyone is searching for love on cupid's day."

"Are you going?" It was a sad Dr. Bob.

"Something tells me I should wait and eat lunch with these guys to start. You know, don't rush into anything. Take my time. I might need to escape from a meal quickly."

"I may try that service myself," said Fay thoughtfully.

Dr. Bob came forward to set the flowers down on the table when he noticed the catalogue.

"Do have a seat," invited Fay politely.

The three of them began to talk amicably about flowers. Soon both women noticed Bob possessed an amazing knowledge of plants. Nancy began to describe her plans for the growing season.

"I could help you get started," said Bob.

Nancy looked at him dismissively.

"No, really," he pleaded. "This isn't a come on. First off, I own half a garage of seed starting supplies at my daughter's house. I keep telling her I'll do something with it, but I never did. If you don't mind Nancy, and you have the space, let's put it to good use. And second, I was hoping to grow plant seedlings for donation."

Bob went on to explain after his wife passed away, he gave their home to his newly divorced daughter to assist with raising his grandchildren. She needed a bigger house and he was content to move into an apartment, except his gardening supplies were in the garage.

"So why don't you grow stuff in her yard?" inquired Nancy.

"I'm afraid I've become a third wheel. I used to spend a lot of time over at the house, but lately she found her own beau to cut her lawn, if you know what I mean."

Fay's eyebrows shot up. "Wait—you planted a lawn?"

Bob appeared guilty. "Umm, the whole xeriscape thing is a rather new interest. I decided I was ready for a radical change."

Bob told them he recently looked at some houses for sale where he could try his low-water ideas, but it didn't feel right to buy a house alone. He and his wife enjoyed taking care of their yard together.

"You could give me advice for my lawn?" asked Fay.

Bob knew all the ins and outs of healthy grass in the Southwest. He suggested complimentary shrubs and flowers. He patiently drew a diagram to explain how Fay could reduce her lawn into zones to use less water. It was a compromise of sorts. He promised she would be far happier with rows of lavender than boring green turf, and she could leave a spot of grass.

"Picture yourself in the south of France," coaxed Bob.

A smile appeared on Fay's lips. "But wouldn't France be just as bad as my lawn?"

"Oh, no."

He went on to explain about some heartier varieties of lavender. She seemed to seriously consider his suggestions.

"I am totally focusing on flowers this year," announced Nancy.

Bob looked down at the table where the two ignored tulips started to wilt.

"Let me get a vase," said Fay, jumping up. She found the perfect white one.

Jane walked in.

Fay turned to Bob, looking at the flowers, "Do you mind?"

With a smile he shook his head.

Nancy stood up. "Here Jane, Bob brought us these two tulips, but we would like you to take them as a thank you for helping bring Fay and me back together."

Jane smiled happily, as if she managed to bring all three of them together for Valentine's Day. "Cupid's work is never done," said Jane, as she left with the vase.

Soon Bob left as well.

Nancy turned to Fay. "I don't care what you say. Jane is a space cadet. California stuff is way too woo-woo for me." Her hands fluttered in the air.

"I shouldn't have said anything at dinner. It's still too soon for you."

"And," said Nancy, shutting out the other woman's last comment, "old women should be more careful about how much they drink."

Nancy abandoned her brew as she made a hasty exit from the tea shop.

CHAPTER 18

Nancy felt fully prepared for her next quilt class. She hoped everyone's design problems were resolved and they could move on to her favorite part— actual quilt stitching of fabric with batting.

When class time rolled around in the evening, her students seemed slow to appear. Bernice was first to arrive, since she was finally in better health. While waiting for the others, Bernice took out several photo transfers she ironed to cloth. Now she needed to figure out which image she wanted to stitch. Nancy left them on the table for the rest of the class to see. She was impressed by Bernice's sharp eye.

Jill came in second with an entire bag of fiber samples made into quilt batting. She was in touch with small production mills across the country, several of which sent her small batches to try out.

She discovered fascinating blends—wools mixed with fibers such as silk, nylon, buffalo, a milk protein, and even exotic qiviut wool. Who knew there was an animal called a muskox?

There was also more complicated batting made with cotton, cashmere, and hemp, plus another featuring cotton, wool, silk and kelp fiber. Jill graciously offered to share her bounty with the rest of the class. She could get feedback about what worked best.

Trish and Keisha arrived next. They both seemed wary of what they produced. Trish still wasn't pleased with her painted fabric design. She admired Bernice's photo prints with envy.

Keisha told her classmates about the Cute Guy episode. When she knocked on his apartment door to explain what happened, he became very angry. Keisha later left the bag of tattered fabrics in front of his door in tears. Her apology went worse than expected, but he didn't take her up on her offer to replace the clothing. Instead, she was quite surprised the next morning to find the bag in front of her door with a couple of his own shirts added to the pile. On top was a note apologizing for his words and encouraging her to do her project. He added something about grabbing coffee in the future and wanting to see her finished work.

Keisha was overwhelmed getting it all together, literally. She ended her story with a huge smile. She turned to Nancy, "Jane was right. I needed to create good energy to meet the Cute Guy."

"Enough of the Jane nonsense," snapped Nancy. "Didn't we hear too much already?"

Keisha stared back, mystified. Nancy realized all the other students were looking at her as well. She was saved by Raleigh as he strutted through the door.

"Hello, famous quilt makers."

"Whatever in the world are you talking about?" asked Trish.

"Have you beautiful women not seen today's newspaper?"

"Who still reads a paper?" wondered Keisha out loud.

Raleigh removed the Albuquerque Journal from his man purse and flipped the paper open to the Metro section. Nancy noted the silver fittings on his bag matched his silver buttons and zippers perfectly. His custom matching leather shoes sported silver buckles. He seemed to excel at dress. She didn't know enough before to appreciate his efforts.

Nancy glanced down and read the blaring headline from halfway across the room—PERFOMER CHARGED WITH OBSCENITY. When Nancy got closer she could make out the smaller print—City Council Ready to Enforce New Ordinance.

Raleigh cleared his throat and began to read out loud, "Performance artist Aen Rant was charged late last night with breaking the city's new obscenity ordinance passed by city council earlier in the week. Lt. Collins, the new city Enforcement Officer, said Albuquerque will no longer tolerate public nuisances disguised as art. The ordinances were passed in reaction to growing public concern about unacceptable displays of lewd content. New councilor Smithe was recently elected on the campaign promise to rid the city of indecency. He cited the example of anatomically correct leather bears, life-size with genital piercings, on display in a storefront window in Nob Hill."

"I love those bears," editorialized Raleigh.

He continued reading, "In the past the city didn't pass any legislation with enough teeth in it to force the owners to remove the bears from the public view of children, said Smithe. The councilor vowed it would change in the future."

"My," said Bernice. "This is a sad day for the city--when people can't make real art anymore because they worry about being prosecuted. Where does the removal end? Who gets to decide what is lewd?" The wrinkled old woman was visibly upset.

Nancy thought to herself Ann and Janice would disagree with Bernice's definition of art and would feel they were protecting their families. At that moment she realized the class started with the two women missing. Were they upset about Aen's banners?

"Your illustrations at Aen's performance worked?" asked Jill. "Or was there more?"

"Knowing Aen, bet there was more," said Trish. "I understand she is trying to prove a point, but she purposely pushes it too far."

"There was a lot more," said Raleigh. "I won't bore you with the rest of the article. Just a bunch of stuffed shirts talking about blah, blah, blah. About how she shouldn't have said some things in her show, inappropriate content and all that. How local theaters should come up with a rating system like the movies. Whatever. Like any of those small minded people ever attend live productions. Like World Wrestling isn't offensive to one's sensibilities."

"So the public outrage isn't just about the banners?" asked Nancy hopefully.

"Well, it mostly was," answered Raleigh. "The banners were what actually broke the new ordinances. Everything else about the performance was just complaints."

"Oh."

"The banners will make good visual evidence in court," said Bernice, in her small voice.

The class turned to look at her.

"It's striking evidence. It gives the prosecutors something large and shocking to present. Everyone in the courtroom will be able to see it."

"At least the quilt shop wasn't mentioned," said Nancy.

"I forgot part of the article," said Raleigh.

Nancy watched in horror as Raleigh traced his finger along the words, stood up, flipped back a couple more pages, and then announced, "Performance artist Aen Rant claimed the banners in question came from a class at Nancy's Quilting located in Downtown Albuquerque. Rant credits the class with inspiring her to create a visual image to express her angst at modern relationships and a metaphor for her grandmother's life."

"I still have no idea what she meant," said Trish.

Raleigh continued, "Rant told the Journal that removing the banners from her performance limits her free speech. Two new shows were added later in the week. Rant anticipates it will be attended by local visual and performance artists, protestors, and civil liberty groups, who say they will make their own signs to replace the banners seized by the police."

"Sounds like they're going to confiscate a bunch of obscene signs to go with the banners," said Jill. "Guess we won't see Aen."

"You ladies are going to the last two performances, right?" asked Raleigh. "I know I'll get my signs ready."

The others murmured excuses, although Bernice seemed open to the suggestion. Little did they know something even bigger would demand their attention. The class continued to talk about the charges filed against Aen. The quilt projects, along with the bag of batting, sat ignored.

The door opened and Ann walked in.

Immediately everyone could see she was crying, and not a little, either. Her face was puffy and her make-up long gone.

Nancy suddenly forgot her anxieties about her quilt shop appearing in the newspaper article. "Oh, my God, has Janice been hurt?"

Ann shook her head. She tried to speak, but broke down in sobs. Trish ran over and wrapped her in a big hug.

When Ann regained her composure and adjusted her glasses, she explained, through tears, Janice's husband Mike was killed two days earlier during a test flight over the Nevada desert. The group heard vaguely about the accident on the news, an explosion in mid-air which happened so quickly there was no time for escape. However, the names of the pilots and crews were not yet released.

Other eyes filled with tears as they listened to Ann describe Janice when she found out. Ann was at her house the last couple days trying to help Janice and the kids cope as best as they could. The quilt class was the first time Ann allowed herself to take a break as Janice's family arrived to get ready for the funeral.

"No work will get done tonight," said Bernice sadly.

Everyone tried to comfort Ann as best they could. Ann explained the two families were next door neighbors for the last three years. She experienced a deep loss herself.

Nancy sat down at the table as conversation swirled around her. She looked at the quilting materials in a pile and deeply wished there was something to comfort Janice.

A cold wind swept through the store, raising the hairs on Nancy's arms. She reflexively grabbed the quilting materials to keep them from blowing away. She then noticed no one else could feel the wind. Only she alone felt the rush of cold air against her skin. None of the fabrics or papers stirred.

"It was so sad," said Ann. "Mike and Janice had a big fight on the morning he left. She feels so bad about it now. She kept saying, over and over again last night, she wished she had the chance to see him once more. She should have told him she loved him."

"Now she'll never get the chance," said Keisha, choking back her own tears.

Silence filled the room.

Nancy thought about Ann more and about how she wanted to grant Janice her one last wish. She put her hands back on the table, next to the materials, and a wind blew hard against her.

Was Nancy going insane? Did the news of Mike's death loosen her grip on reality? Clearly no one else felt a strong breeze. Nancy brought up her arms and hugged herself tight. The wind faded.

Nancy looked around at the others. The group was still engrossed in comforting Ann and helping her talk through what Janice might need in the way of assistance. Everyone wanted to volunteer.

Nancy slowly put her hands back on the table. She could feel a breeze stirring, and when she moved her hands over the fabrics she was struck by a strong wind. She stood and felt herself lean into the table to stand upright, yet the materials didn't blow away, and no one else in the room noticed.

****

Nancy went directly to Fay's house after the class. Normally she would call ahead, but nothing was normal at this point.

Nancy asked, as the front door opened, "There is something really spooky about Gold Street, right?"

"Did you want to talk about the dinner conversation at Garcia's?"

"No, I don't."

"Okay, so why are you here?" Fay tried to ask in a delicate manner as she pulled her robe tight. Nancy didn't seem to want to come inside and she wasn't dressed to go out.

"You people are freaks," Nancy blurted out. She turned, as if ready to run away.

"Did something happen today?"

"Yes."

"You look upset, dear."

Nancy's eyes filled with tears as she turned back to face Fay. "My student's husband died."

"Why don't I get dressed and we can head to the tea shop? I can make just the thing."

Nancy froze. "Your tea isn't normal. Why didn't I think of that before?"

Fay waited patiently at the door.

"You don't make regular tea, do you?" Nancy's voice began to climb.

"No, dear. I don't brew a standard assortment of teas."

"You make weird tea!" Nancy shouted into the night. Her world was coming undone. The ground beneath her feet would surely tilt at any moment. It was like her life came unglued.

Maybe she was actually mentally ill.

Fay decided to put modesty aside and stepped out on to her front walk. She put her arms around Nancy and pulled in her in a close, tight hug.

"I'm sorry. You're taking this badly. I just didn't know the right time to tell you about Gold Street. I wanted to for a while now, but it's not easy to explain. I didn't think you would believe me."

Nancy pulled away from the embrace.

"I don't believe you! This place is nuts. I need to get away."

She turned and ran down the sidewalk. Fay called out after her, "I'm here when you're ready to talk." She added under her breath, "You need to learn to use your gift. Don't run away from it."

CHAPTER 19

Nancy's Quilting didn't open the next day.

Nancy's alarm couldn't be heard over the extra sleeping pill she took the night before. She dreamed she fell into a black tunnel. The emptiness scared her and she tried to escape. She grabbed rocks, tore apart beautiful bunches of flowers and tried to catch a furry animal, but nothing could prevent slow sinking into a deep hole. Nothing.

The ground started to swallow her. She couldn't breathe. Her chest sank heavily as she gasped for air.

Nancy's eyes popped open.

"Tompkins!" she said with a start. "Get off my chest." She gave the annoyed cat a hard push. He slowly rolled over.

As she waited for the fog to clear from her head, she reassured herself every single thing in life was backed by a rational explanation. One just needed to be awake and aware. She could figure out any root cause for strange happenings.

She jumped out of bed when she realized it was already almost noon. Long past Tompkins' breakfast time and his mid-morning snack. Nancy threw on sweats and headed to the kitchen.

Her answering machine blinked with quite a few messages. She forwarded her cell phone to her home phone last night to avoid calls for a while. Oh, bother. She also now remembered she arranged a coffee date with an interesting man from the dating service at 10 AM. Unlikely she could salvage that one.

Beep: This is Stan. Just wanted to confirm we're meeting later this morning at the Flying Star Café Downtown. I'm really looking forward to getting to know you.

Beep: This is Stan again. I can't seem to find you. I'm wearing the expensive Italian brown jacket. I'm a bit worried you confused the location. Did you mistakenly go to the Flying Star in Nob Hill? Just give me a buzz back and let me know where you are.

Beep: Stan again. Maybe you thought it was the Flying Star on the Westside? Or the Northeast Heights? No hard feelings. Just give me a call back.

Beep: Nancy, dear, this is Fay. I know you experienced a rough night. Please give me a call back when you get the chance. We should talk.

Beep: Stan again. Remember me? Apparently not. So maybe you think this is funny. Maybe you think forcing some guy to show up and wait around for you is a real laugh. It's already an hour past our meeting time.

Beep: My ex-wife was a total loser like you and always did this to me. Do you hags think you can mess with men?

Beep: Oh, and don't worry about opening the quilt shop. I put a note on the door and if anyone needs something, they can leave a message with me at the tea store.

Beep: However, I must say you attracted rather unusual people to your store window this morning. And a reporter. Is there anything odd going on? I hope you're alright.

Yes, thought Nancy, weird things are going on.

Beep: I don't know why I even try with you stupid hags. You are all the same. Sluts every one of you. You think you can treat a man like dirt and we'll show up for more? Do I look stupid? Am I wearing a sign that says kick me?

Beep: The reporter just came into the tea shop and asked if I would like to make a statement about the obscenity charges. Nancy, dear—did your class make lewd quilts? I didn't think to ask about the subject matter when I offered to host an exhibit at my gallery space. I thought your students would make little birds and flowers. Or something like that...

Beep: Bob here. Fay said you could use some cheering up today. You might be a bit under the weather, but ready to start your seedlings. I'll be by in a jiffy with some planting supplies.

Beep: Don't bother calling me back with your sorry-ass excuses. I heard every lie in the book from you hags. You would suck a man dry if you could. I'm glad now you didn't show up. Saves me from hearing your pathetic whine. You just want to toy with me like I'm a mouse. That's all you women ever want. Just to tease and tease. I would probably waste my money buying you coffee. Don't contact me again.

Like I would, thought Nancy. What a narrow escape. She felt lucky to sleep through her coffee date. She made a mental note to contact the dating service and warn them. She should play back his messages for them to hear.

Beep: I totally forgot. Bob stopped by. He noticed the quilt shop was closed and I told him you were at home ready to start your planting today. He should be there soon. You are home, right?

Beep: And I have a pile of messages for you. I won't read through most of them. Really odd requests. Like do you carry erotic fabrics? Whatever that means. The reporter left her contact info in case you want to make a statement. And a rather attractive mature police officer, who says he's been in your store before, said he needs to check your inventory when you open again to make sure you don't display any merchandise in violation of the new city obscenity ordinances. You don't, do you? I can run over and hide things, if you need. Although I can't think of anything law-breaking in your shop.

Beep: Made a stop at the garden store. Will pick up lunch along the way and be there soon. Hope I'm not taking too long.

Beep: So I just have to ask--do you know the police officer who just left the tea store? He was rather charming, if you like men in uniform, although I never have. Perhaps I should give it a second thought. Maybe I shouldn't have sent Bob to your place?

A text flashed across Nancy's cell phone from Theresa M — U OK? Nancy hit K in return.

Beep: Dear, we really do need to talk. Come by the tea shop tonight after close. No one will see you enter from the alley. Oh, and do you carry bondage equipment, like straps and leather? I wouldn't think so, but I was asked the question several times this morning.

Nancy startled at a knock on her front door. She wore sweats and barely combed her hair before she opened to Bob. So much for Keisha's fabulous make-over. Bob still looked pleased to see her.

Bob offered to set up on her sun porch, but Nancy said it was fine to bring the gardening supplies into the kitchen. She skipped the last two meals, so her sink was clean.

Bob pulled out a Middle Eastern meal from a brown paper bag: hummus, falafels, warm pita bread, olives and sauces. Nancy lost herself in the spicy aromas.

"No offense," said Bob, "but you look like death warmed over." He added out of politeness, "I mean, seems like a rough night. The flu? In general, I think you've looked fabulous lately. Really nice. Want to talk about it?"

"I don't know," replied Nancy. "It's not much fun to sit and listen to someone go through a laundry list of problems."

"Doesn't seem like a regular day for you. I doubt this is normal. Really, I'm a great listener."

They ate their lunch in silence as Nancy tried to collect her thoughts. Getting some calories in her body would help. Bob waited patiently. He wouldn't push her and would sit respectfully until she was ready.

She realized she wasn't used to someone respectful of her needs. She didn't have to make conversation to amuse him. She didn't have to jabber constantly to fill the empty air. With Bob she could mull over a situation. Thinking back, she's always entertained her ex-husband. He couldn't stand contemplation, or, in retrospect, her thinking about herself.

As they unpacked the supplies, she finally spoke about the last couple days, except for the ridiculous stuff about magic on Gold Street. She didn't want him thinking she was a lunatic.

She worried aloud to him about what the public was going to think of the quilt shop after Aen's stunt with the lewd banners. She did mention what a great artist Raleigh was. Bob assured her she might be surprised at what the publicity generated. Once a guy was shot in front of his vet clinic. It was horrible, but brought him some new clients after they saw his clinic on the evening news.

Reassured, Nancy went through a list of her anxieties. Was she going to be able to get a niche product off the ground to make her store profitable? Was opening a money pit instead of buying a retirement condo in Arizona a mistake? Would she adjust to life in Albuquerque?

She patted the planting soil down so hard as she spoke the plastic sides split open. Bob gently took both of her hands.

It was a long time since a man softly caressed her hands. For a while he didn't speak, lightly stroking her skin in a calming manner. Nancy could see how he would do well working with animals. He communicated through his touch. She instinctively knew he would be an amazing lover.

Bob broke the silence with his deep and soothing voice. "The store is making you worried and upset?"

"No," said Nancy, and suddenly burst out with deep, heavy sobs. It was just as well she hadn't applied any make-up.

He moved around the table and enveloped her in his arms. Her head rested on his shoulder as he pulled her tightly in. She breathed in his musky odor as she tried to calm. His body relaxed. She found herself following his physical lead. He gently swayed them both and her tears slowed to a trickle.

He made no demands, gave no advice, didn't even try to get her to stop crying. He simply held on. Nancy realized he was content to stay that way as long as she needed. His schedule wasn't important. He would give as long as she needed.

Not like her ex-husband Bobby.

She gasped out loud while looking him directly in the face. Why hadn't the thought occurred to her before?

"Did I startle you? I'm sorry."

"No, it's just you have the same exact name as my husband. I mean, my ex."

"Bob is an excellent name. You have great taste."

She giggled in spite of herself. He eased them back against the counter and hugged tighter. She noticed he briefly grimaced. She realized they weren't standing in the most comfortable position for him.

She broke away to lead him to her living room couch. Without words, he sat down and she climbed into his arms. They snuggled into a comfortable position as he gently rocked her back and forth. It didn't matter how long they stayed in the same comforting position, he was prepared to give her whatever she wanted.

Her marriage was never that way. Maybe young lovers were always in a rush, but Nancy never felt acceptance of her needs. She didn't hold her ex-husband's attention for long. She never thought about it much before, but looking back, she was always trying to measure up in his eyes, like she wasn't enough. She constantly tried to make her marriage right, buying new dresses or cooking elaborate romantic dinners. She always searched for something, a new hair style or sexier shoes, which would make herself special.

After she divorced, she gave up on herself, until Keisha's make-over got her out of her rut. It forced her to think about herself as a desirable woman again. What was she hiding behind in her baggy jeans and frumpy sweaters? She could pretend that it just didn't matter.

Here, in Bob's arms, wearing old sweats, she realized she didn't need to do anything extra for him. He was happy to spend time with her as she was.

However, she wanted to look and feel her best with him, not because she had to, but because it was fun to dress up for dates. She wanted to look like a successful business owner, because she was going to fake it until she made it, so to speak.

Nancy's mind wandered back to her ex-husband Bobby. She felt deep grief at the loss of her marriage and now he was dying of cancer. How could she still feel so bad this many years later?

Fresh tears spilled down her cheeks.

"Do you want to talk about it? But you don't have to..."

His deep voice caressed her in such a gentle manner.

Nancy explained about her student Janice's husband dying suddenly and how it was forcing her to confront her fears that her ex-husband would soon also die. Except that she kept trying to suppress it because they weren't married any longer. She was replaced by a second wife a long time ago. She didn't have a right to her lonely grief, did she? She should be over it, no longer a part of his life. Did her thoughts even make sense?

Bob, in turn, talked about his wife's death. Emotions he hadn't expressed to anyone. He reflected on his marriage, so many years ago, to have a young daughter and new big mortgage, while opening his own vet clinic at the same time. How scared he was of failing and his family losing everything. He'd never told his wife about his fears, getting into arguments over little things instead. He wanted her to see him as strong and capable. Bob regretted those petty fights now.

Bob pulled Nancy closer into his arms on the couch and wrapped her up tightly. They sat silently for a couple minutes, until he gently stroked the hair away from her neck and slowly, ever so delicately, started to kiss her with whisper soft lips.

She felt her breath suck in. She lost herself in the depths of his blue eyes. She tried to place the color. Were they a sky blue? No, not really. An ocean blue? No, they seemed earthier and had flecks of color. His eyes were more like a Lapis Lazuli stone, strong and precious.

She felt like she was awakening from a long dream. She pictured some of the cartoon fairy tales she used to watch in her childhood, Disney-type films where the prince awakens the charming maiden from her deep slumber. She understood the feeling. She experienced a sexual reawakening of feelings, desires long dormant inside.

Except she glanced down at her hand and was momentarily surprised to see it covered in wrinkles. When had it happened? How her body changed so much from the time when she actually was a desirable young woman? She suddenly became self-conscious.

"What's wrong?" asked Bob, pulling himself back some from their embrace. He searched her face until he caught her eyes. Just as quickly, she glanced away again.

Nancy brought her arms up around to hug her body. She was suddenly aware of being in her sweats and not putting on a bra. Thank heaven Keisha talked her into throwing away all of her old underwear. The only sexy thing she had on was a pair of red lace undies with a cute bow.

"I look horrible," she said. "I was trying to look better. I must resemble death warmed over today."

"No, beautiful. You don't realize how appealing you are in this moment."

He tugged on her shirt and said in a husky voice, "However, if it would make you feel better, you are welcome to take this off. I wouldn't mind one bit."

She playfully slapped his hand away, while muttering, "I'm sure."

Bob backed away from Nancy to sit back on the couch. With one hand he gently stroked the strands of her hair.

"So is this what you tell all the women?" she asked. She meant to make light conversation, but the words escaping her lips sounded rather harsh. She glanced at his face trying to read his expression.

She began to panic a little. Did she mess up? Was he offended? It dawned on her a tendency to close herself off from her real desires. Could she change?

"Nan," said Bob. "Can I call you Nan? I'd rather be less formal, if you don't mind."

"Sure, no one has ever called me Nan before." Her heart skipped a beat. He already picked a special pet name for her.

"Nan, I have to tell you it's been a long time since I've been with a woman. Well, a new woman, that is."

He scrunched up his face, obviously doing some timeline calculations in his head.

"Since my wife died, I have gone out on some casual dates. Nothing ever progressed beyond a dinner or movies. Certainly I haven't been with a woman trying to talk her into taking off her clothes in many years. Why, not since my wife and I were kids in college."

He laughed at the memory.

"Finally this winter I realized I was tired of walking around my apartment and talking to my animals alone. My daughter is doing fine with our vet practice, and she and the kids have a promising man who would make a wonderful husband and father. They just don't need me like they used to."

He shifted in his seat and continued.

"Okay, to be honest, I think I was starting to get a bit underfoot at her house. My daughter suggested it was time to find some hobbies. Learning about xeriscaping has been fun, but it's not the same as companionship."

"So you're ready for something more?"

"I think I am. I mean, I don't want an instant new wife. I'm not looking to replace her. I know that I never can, but I think I'm realizing there is an empty space in my life I would like to fill."

"Wow," she replied. "I have been so focused on myself I haven't really thought about what your life must have been like the last couple years."

"Well, Nan, my life got a lot sunnier this winter when I met you and Fay."

A dark surge of jealousy stabbed at her heart. It arrived out of nowhere with an ugly pierce.

She jumped off the couch to pace the floor. He looked up at her in amazement.

"What have I done wrong?"

She slowed down to think more calmly. She decided she needed to ask the question which was eating at her for the last few weeks. Better to know the truth now before anything else happened between them.

"Do you wish I was Fay?"

"What are you talking about?"

"Was Fay your first choice? Go ahead, you can tell me. I would rather know. Do you wish you were sitting here with Fay instead of me?"

"That's absurd."

"No, it's not."

"Why would you ask me such a question?"

She spun around to face him. "See, you're avoiding answering my question. Just like I thought."

"God," he said, running his hand through his hair. "I can't believe we're having an argument."

Her eyes narrowed at him.

"Nan, please sit down." He patted the couch. "Please," he asked again with pleading eyes. "I'm not very good at this. I never was. If my wife were here she would tell you herself."

Suddenly she realized Bob was spending more time thinking about his past than any future woman in his life. She let out a long breath of air and sat down beside him.

"Fay is a friend?" he asked.

"Yeah," she admitted. Okay, if she really thought back over the last couple days, Fay was a friend of deep and loving kindness. She sent Bob to her house to comfort her.

"Fay is a wonderful person," she said quietly. "I guess that's why I'm so jealous of her. You know she's lovely with excellent personal style. Her house is a showcase, very immaculate inside."

"I have a bunch of little critters. How do you think they would get along in her house? Do you think Fay has ever owned a pet weasel who likes to claw the curtains and climb across the counter?"

Nancy burst out laughing. She could see his point.

"Nan, you're the person I've really noticed from the beginning. I'm a homebody who loves my animals. I seem to get along better with them than lots of people. I like a quiet evening at home with my books. I don't think I'd be much use at the parties Fay has described holding."

"Oh, yes, she has wonderful parties," Nancy replied without paying too much attention to what she was saying. She was leaning over to plant a deep kiss on his lips.

"You make me remember I'm a man."

Nancy knew what he meant. She pictured them at that moment as Adam and Eve in the garden—the only two people in the world, with lots of creatures, of course.

She pressed her body against his. She could feel their aging bodies, her stomach layers against his soft gut. She traced the wrinkles around his eyes with her fingers.

He stopped talking to search her face. "Nan, you make me feel in a way that I haven't felt in a very long time. Please know."

She gathered her courage and led him to her bedroom. They stared into each other's eyes for a few minutes before they quietly began to undress each other. She took him to a place he hadn't been in a long time. It felt special. He looked like an excited child unwrapping the largest present under the Christmas tree. His smile lit up the room. She wondered if she had ever felt this cherished by a lover.

Afterwards, he cuddled her gently in his arms while whispering about how fantastic she made him feel. The afternoon hours began to slip away as they both drifted into a contented sleep.

****

Later, Nancy awoke as Bob stirred. She started to pull away, but he drew her closer again, eyes still closed with a smile.

She deeply inhaled his musky scent. With no words, she traced his scratchy five-o'clock shadow across his chin. He opened his eyes continuing to grin.

As if in a trance, he slowly moved his face toward hers. She closed her eyes and soon felt his delicious lips starting to taste hers in a deep kiss. His five o'clock shadow bristled against her cheek.

Five o'clock.

Nancy shot up straight, startling Bob.

"I need to get to Fay's tea shop. It's about closing time and I need to get over there."

She apologized as best she could. In the kitchen they surveyed the mess. He started to clean up, but she suggested he leave it. They could work on planting on Monday. She wouldn't use her kitchen much in the meanwhile anyway.

He reluctantly left with another kiss.

CHAPTER 20

Nancy owned a key to the Downtown Tea Shop & Gallery. She quietly let herself in the back. She wasn't ready to face the quilt shop yet. She tried to collect her thoughts. The world spun too quickly. Everything she thought she knew was changing.

Fay emerged a few minutes later. She set down cups of steaming brew. Nancy bent forward and took a couple of sniffs.

"You always drank my tea before."

"I was never suspicious of what was in it."

"Never? And you don't trust me now?"

"I don't know what to think."

Fay settled in a chair to sip her tea and wait. Nancy finally sighed and took a drink. Familiar warmth filled her body and she began to relax.

"Why didn't you tell me anything before?"

"Because you weren't ready. You wouldn't believe me. You needed to experience the magic for yourself."

"You could warn me!"

"Did you enjoy your visit with Bob today?"

"What does that have to do with anything?"

"Did the two of you chat? I would think you both have a lot in common."

"Okay, we talked all afternoon. About everything under the sun. I'm so comfortable with Bob. I don't think there's anything I couldn't tell him."

"How about the magic on Gold Street?"

"We can talk about everything in the world... but that. I just couldn't bring it up. He would think I'm a complete nutcase."

"Exactly."

Nancy conceded the other woman's point. She told Bob almost everything she thought today, except the strange powers of Gold Street.

"Am I losing my mind?" asked Nancy.

"I know this will be hard to accept, but each store on this block has its own potential for a touch of magic. Nothing huge or earth shattering. Well, Jane seems a little more connected to the other side—if you know what I mean."

"Jane is a weirdo. A complete freak of nature."

"I can see you'll find a little more difficulty with Jane. She's the only one who can communicate with the spirit of Madame Beesley."

"The landlady who used to own this block of buildings?"

"I think she would argue she still gets a say in what goes on around here."

"Great. I opened a haunted quilt store. It must be the only one in the country. Maybe I'll make a big tourist sign to put out front. Charge them ten dollars admission to walk in and see the ghosts."

"It doesn't work that way. I said your store will receive a touch. Most of the owners discover their special gift when they work on something they love to do. They create a special moment or power. It needs to be done in the service of someone else with an open and loving heart. You personally won't gain anything from it."

"Well, that's just jolly."

Fay gave the other woman a few minutes to absorb the information. Nancy slowly sipped her tea and set her cup down.

"Your special brews help me relax and feel okay about the world."

"Not a huge thing, but I enjoy sharing it. Notice I never charge you for my comfort teas. The magic can't be sold. Ever since I was a little girl, I liked to hold tea parties more than any of my friends. The other girls would set out some dishes willy-nilly for their dolls and bears, but not me. I held extravaganzas."

"I can only imagine."

"I could spend days preparing for a doll tea event. I would make my older sister help me gather wild flowers to decorate our room, and my younger brother became waiter."

"What inspired you?"

Fay thought for a while.

She seemed to drift, lost in another time. Nancy began to wonder if she was distracted and forgot the question, but then she seemed to return.

"I never made this connection before, but the last memory of my father at home, before he shipped out during World War II, was patting me on the head and telling me to have a tea party ready for him. He said, 'Sweet Pea, we'll have a dandy celebration when I come back.' And then he left."

"Did you?"

"No, he never came home."

Fay never talked to Nancy about her father.

"At first, I thought my mother would never be happy ever again. After the war ended, we still needed to use war ration coupons for a while, although products began to reappear on the empty store shelves. One day, I splurged extra coupons to buy a big bag of sugar. Luckily, the rationing would end soon. Somewhere I found fresh lemons and made my family the most delicious pitchers of real lemonade with a month's worth of wartime sugar. What an extravagance. I added fresh lavender."

Fay smiled at the memory.

"My mother was delighted with the drink. We hoped it meant maybe better times would come around the corner. You see, everyone was worried the Great Depression would start again after the war ended. My mother didn't know how we would get by if that happened, but she allowed herself to indulge in my lemonade. It was the closest thing to happiness I saw in her in a very long time."

Fay stopped abruptly and studied Nancy.

"You were given some sort of gift at your store, too. You just need to figure out what it is."

"How would I know?"

"Did you feel a breeze stirring?"

"More like a wind."

"Some people are so obtuse." Nancy jumped at the sound of Jane's voice. It was like Jane came out of nowhere during their discussion.

"Do you always sneak up on people?"

Nancy hoped Jane didn't hear her earlier comments.

Fay left the back room to get a third cup of tea. Nancy avoided eye contact with Jane. She would prefer to leave herself. She wanted to put as much distance between herself and Jane as possible.

"Are you running an erotic quilt shop?" asked Jane.

Nancy put her head down on the desk. So far, she managed to avoid thinking about it.

Fay returned. "Here Nancy, I brought you another cup of tea as well. Drink up." She gave Jane the evil eye.

"Fine," said Jane, "I just thought I'd pop by and help Nancy along on her journey. I noticed the energy around the quilt shop was quite strong since the Thursday evening class. Obviously, it's time for a little magic to begin, although perhaps the space should be cleansed first. I saw the oddest collection of people out front."

"No one was inside the quilt store today," Fay informed Jane. "It stayed closed. Nancy wasn't feeling well."

"That's better. But still, you attract really off-kilter energies right now. After this little pow-wow, we'll go over and burn an incense to clear the air to get your magic going in a productive direction. Otherwise, who knows what your new energy field will attract."

"That's just too weird," said Nancy.

"You may not believe me, but you will thank me later. So what is your gift?" asked Jane.

"I don't know."

Jane proceeded to quiz Nancy. When did she feel a breeze, or wind in her case, what was she doing? What was she thinking about? Nancy described the quilting projects laid out on the table and her desire to grant Janice's last wish to see her husband one more time.

Jane sat down on the top of the desk and folded her arms and legs. She appeared to be one of Rachel's yoga students. She sat deep in concentration for a while.

The other two women sipped their tea quietly so they would not disturb her.

Jane finally opened her eyes slowly.

"I think I figured it out."

"Madame Ghost didn't tell you directly?"

Fay shot Nancy a dirty look.

"Your student can get her wish to see her dead husband one more time. However, such a big thing takes a lot of work to happen. His spirit likely didn't move on yet, but you need to do something to bring him to the quilt shop."

"What?" asked Nancy and Fay in unison.

"From your descriptions I'm guessing you need to get your class to sew their projects into a big quilt together. All of their energies bound together for her to use."

"You guess?" blurted out Nancy. "Making a full quilt takes a long time. What if you're wrong? What if we miss his spirit and follow some kind of wild goose chase?" She began to pace. "And how do I talk my students into giving up their individual projects they all worked so long and hard on? What do I tell them? And must I use Aen's banners? They're currently in police lock-up. However, Janice wouldn't appreciate them in her quilt."

Jane didn't look the least bit concerned.

"You'll figure out the details. We need to go now and cleanse the quilt shop space to prepare."

CHAPTER 21

Monday morning Nancy discovered Bob was an early riser. She vowed she would look more presentable the next time he arrived at the house, however, she forgot to set her alarm. She roused at his knocks on the front door, as the faintest rays of sunlight streaked in soft yellows across the sky.

With a moan she rolled out of bed to answer the door wearing her dingy old terry robe. Bob ignored her disheveled state and told her that he could set up for their seed planting. She excused herself as quickly as possible. Tompkins hadn't stirred from bed.

The old Nancy would have hastily thrown on some ragged clothes. The improved Nancy took her time to jump in the shower and relax before getting dressed. She rummaged through her dresser until she found the fresh crisp silk shirt she recently purchased. She threw on her stylish jeans. She couldn't wait to show Bob the sexy v-line that flattered her bust. The old Nancy would balk at wasting new clothes on gardening. Her new self felt confident in her sex appeal.

She spent extra time fixing her hair and applying just the right amount of make-up. She felt comfortable in her own skin when she walked into the kitchen.

Nancy gasped in surprise. Bob turned from the stove to give her a wink. "Hope you don't mind that I'm making you breakfast. I love to cook."

She inhaled the wonderful aromas as she inspected the supplies he had brought into the house. He must have realized she lived like a young bachelor—half a loaf of bread and a jar of peanut butter in the fridge, plus a quart of spoiled milk. She often got by on a can of soup which she heated in the microwave for dinner.

Bob stirred, grated, chopped and stirred some more. With his attention on the stove, she could watch the muscles in his arms flex as he threw some fresh vegetable slices into the pan. A sweet butter aroma wafted off his sauté.

He removed a pan of biscuits he was baking from the oven. She hadn't been sure that the oven actually worked. Apparently it did, as she was greeted by the most tantalizing smell of fresh bread. She grew almost dizzy anticipating the soft, moist texture of butter melting down the sides of the biscuits.

A different scent beckoned her as she spotted thick strips of bacon cooling on the drain board. She was tempted to steal a piece to taste its salty crispness. Finally she picked out one more scent of the warm aroma of freshly brewing coffee. She listened to the drip from the machine.

She stood rapt as he started cracking open eggs. Saliva filled her mouth in anticipation. She slowly licked her lips.

"Nan, why don't you go through my grocery bags to find the condiments? I hope I remembered everything you like."

Reaching around she first pulled out a specialty cinnamon-flavored cream to add to their coffee, along with raw sugar. The mix of the two appealed to her, although she never tried this particular combo.

She rooted around the bags some more until she came up with a couple of jars.

"I didn't know which you would prefer on your biscuits," he explained.

She studied the two packages. One contained raspberry preserves made locally with red chile, while the other was a wild clover blossom honey. How would she choose?

"I don't know," she said. "Maybe we need to try them both out." She gave him a mischievous grin. "I think I prefer the chile."

His smile was equally wicked. "I've always like honey myself."

Later, she was left wondering how she managed before meeting Bob. He stirred passions she had left dormant for far too long. What other delights was she missing?

Eventually they got around to finishing their meal.

****

Despite their morning adventures, they still managed to plant plenty of seeds. Bob shared a wealth of information about growing flowers in the Southwest. He walked around her yard to show her the changing light and explain about hard clay soil.

She hired a professional landscaper for the next day. She realized she would need a lot of help to build raised flower beds to fill with soil for a variety of plants. Bob and she exchanged emails about what she might like in her yard.

dogfix1: You have a lot of space. Do you want to leave room for a hammock in addition to the other seating areas?

quiltgrrl: I'm not semi-retired like you. I don't have time to lounge around.

dogfix1: You're breaking my heart. Maybe you should slow down.

quiltgrrl: And give up what?

dogfix1: Good point. You haven't mentioned any pets beyond Tompkins. Do you need a dog run? (Too bad they don't make cat runs. He could use it.)

quiltgrrl: I'm not home enough to care for a dog. Bummer. I used to have a small farm with animal rescue space back in Indiana.

dogfix1: You said the right words! I do animal rescue, except I don't have any space at my apartment. Okay, beyond a couple birds, an adorable weasel who would like to eat the birds, and some goldfish. Would you believe someone abandoned goldfish on the door step of the vet clinic? But don't tell my landlord. You'll get me evicted.

quiltgrrl: I don't have time to rescue animals, remember? Should I install automatic sprinklers so my plants get watered?

dogfix1: Great idea. Underground irrigation saves water. No wasted evaporation. What if you had help with the rescue animals?

Nancy didn't answer the last email. What was Bob really asking? Did she want to know the answer?

****

Bob didn't bring up the subject of rescue animals or spending regular time at Nancy's house when they ate brunch together on Wednesday. Maybe he sensed it was too soon. They met at a great little place Downtown called Café Lush.

At the restaurant Nancy read the menu over three times trying to decide what she wanted. Everything looked so delicious. The owners lived in the area and used local farm ingredients. Should she order the breakfast burrito with house-made green chile sausage, a breakfast pizza of potato crust topped with eggs, local cheese, and green chile, or their specialty of Lushaladas—stacked enchiladas with chile, cheese, and breakfast potatoes topped with two eggs?

She couldn't resist the Lushaladas. Bob ordered the same. During the meal he described to her all the changes he observed Downtown in the past thirty years at his vet clinic, both good times and decline, although Downtown appeared to be back on the upswing.

He also talked about his daughter joining him in his business after she finished vet school. He never lectured or gave Nancy unsolicited advice about her own business, but he patiently listened as she described the challenges she faced with her store in great detail. He offered to introduce her to people he knew who might be able to help.

However, she didn't need as much assistance right now. Aen's banner publicity brought all kinds of people to the quilt shop. For the first couple days they were rather dicey, but slowly actual quilters began to show up. Several said they had no idea about her store until they saw the news. Did Jane's purification ritual cleanse the store after all?

Or not?

Was she out of the woods yet? Her revenue was picking up, but would the increased sales last? Everyone warned her that retail goes in cycles. She needed to prepare for the inevitable slow winters ahead.

She barely noticed as an unfamiliar man reached over to shake Bob's hand. Nancy let her mind drift as the two men exchanged pleasantries.

"So is this the gal you took hiking up to the Gila?" asked the stranger.

Bob's face flushed red.

The man continued undeterred. "I heard you two make a sweet couple. My wife says the camping trip last month was a blast. Was the weather warm enough down there? I hear it's unbelievably hot by summer. You probably went at just the right time. You should come over for dinner one of these days to tell us all about it." He walked away with a smile.

It took every ounce of willpower for Nancy not to scream. When she could finally manage her inside voice she asked, "What overnight trip to the mountains?"

He shifted uncomfortably in his seat. "One of my lady friends and I went on a hiking trip recently."

"Lady friends?"

"Right. Look Nan, I never said I don't spend time with other friends."

"That's what you call it?"

She could feel she would lose her composure. Why did he tell her she was the first person he was intimate with since the death of his wife? Why did she naively believe him without waiting to meet some of his friends and find out more about him? How could she make such stupid mistakes? She may as well be sixteen years old again. A grown woman should be smarter.

She threw the snarled pieces of tissue down in haste as she ran out the door. She knew he couldn't follow immediately after her since he still needed to pay the bill.

The quilt shop was located on the other side of Downtown. She decided to turn the ten minute walk into more of a meander. Her mind was too jumbled with confusing emotions to open the store right now.

The air was pleasantly warm. She tried to focus on the blue skies and bright sunshine.

Her mood failed to improve. She purposely sought out the most derelict areas of Downtown. She trudged past windows which sat empty for decades, their for rent signs curling under the harsh desert sun.

She walked along the abandoned pedestrian mall, hemmed in by the harshness of sheer cliffs of skyscrapers which stood as fortresses against the street. The shade of a sparse stand of trees only served to add gloom. A bum walked by and asked for change as she inhaled the scent of stale urine.

She made her way to the concrete expanse of wasteland known as Civic Plaza. She shuffled out to the Plaza's center. A few people passed on the perimeter where shade blocked the harshness of the sun, but no one came near her.

She knew she must look crazy. She felt the urge to spin in circles to calm her mind. She fought the strong urge to run and not ever look back.

Where would she go? She already decided she should stay put in Albuquerque and keep the store. She would walk over to open soon, but not just yet.

How could Bob treat her this way? How could she let him?

Janice's advice slowly came back to her. Did she have the capacity to love?

Of course, this was entirely his fault. She didn't do anything wrong.

Or did she?

Okay, she would concede she got involved too quickly. But taking it slow didn't change anything when men were cheats and liars. How was she supposed to use her capacity to love if the person on the other side was a rat? Why did she develop a thing for the worst men?

She decided to walk around the perimeter of the plaza to mull over the situation. She found exercise always helped her think better. Guess she didn't get enough of it lately.

Why didn't she ever learn anything about love no matter how old she became?

She heard the sound of her mother's voice—it takes two to tango.

Wasn't that what her mom always said when she got into fights with her siblings? Her mother refused to take sides in any argument because she reasoned that nobody was perfect and everyone contributed to a squabble.

Well, she was rightfully mad when she found out he courted other women. Why take someone on an overnight trip if you won't have sex?

Once Nancy said the words out loud she realized that nobody ever actually said Bob slept with the woman. Okay, it was a reasonable assumption. Yet, didn't she once go with a guy friend on a two day tour? They shared a room but not the bed. When she thought back, Nancy could remember other similar trips.

Maybe she jumped to conclusions without getting all the facts. If Bob's friends wanted to invite her to dinner, she could find out for herself. She would demand she meet some of his lady friends. She would know the real truth quickly.

Nancy walked a couple laps around the plaza and thought about Janice's advice on the capacity to love. She wouldn't forgive Bob if she found out he lied. She wasn't a door mat. However, maybe she should work harder on figuring out if she could fall in love rather than run away. She needed to give love a real chance.

When she got finally opened the quilt shop, Bob was waiting for her.

"I'm sorry Nan. After you left I realized how the camping trip must sound."

Nancy eyed him wearily. "I have a habit of falling for the wrong men. Since coming to Albuquerque I vowed things would be different, but then you turned out to be just like all the others."

"No, you're making the assumption all men are the same. You ran off without giving me a chance to explain. You won't give us a chance. The camping trip was with my departed wife's best friend. Everyone said what a cute couple we would make. My wife remarked how similar we were while she was alive."

"You gave it a try?" Nancy felt her heart soften. Even if they were once together, she might find a way to forgive him for being less than honest about their relationship. Maybe they loved each other from afar for years.

"No, we didn't give it a try. We never wanted to. My wife was correct. We are too much alike to ever be together romantically."

"Oh."

"We went away together to finally talk about some things after my wife's death. Our friend knew the marriage wasn't what it should have been in the last years. I really needed someone to confide in. She was very understanding and helped me see I did my best by sticking with my wife and being there when she needed me the most. She's an important friend to me."

"Oh."

He took a deep breath and turned to face her. "When I met you I thought I found someone truly interested in me. I mean, you seem to enjoy my company. Was I wrong? You got mad awfully fast."

He turned to leave. She grabbed his arm to stop him.

"I don't only want to have sex with you," she blurted out. "I wanted to meet someone special, too. How did this get so confusing all of a sudden? I like you."

A smile slowly spread across his lips, although the deep lines furrowed across his face made him look twenty years older.

She searched his face. "Your wife was sick a long time, wasn't she?"

"Oh God, yes, rest her soul. She really suffered."

They stood silent for a few minutes.

Finally, he spoke. "I won't push you anymore, Nan."

She felt her chest contract. "You're not about to give me the let's be friends talk are you?"

"No, but let's not push it. Maybe we got involved too fast. I think we need to slow down some. I almost wish I could roll back time. We got together when you had too much to think about already."

"You didn't like it?" She was hurt.

He embraced her tightly. "This conversation just keeps getting worse. I didn't mean I didn't enjoy being with you physically. I waited years to feel that with a woman again. What I mean is — let's go back and start again. Would you give me a fresh start?"

"What did you have in mind?"

"How about an old-fashioned date?"

She nodded yes.

"Okay, so I noticed you own a bike. I know some great rides around Downtown and along the trail in the Bosque. There are tables where we could stop for a picnic lunch. I know a freeway overpass where bats fly out at dusk..."

Nancy lost herself in the snuggle as she listened to him describe a picnic outing. She decided it was time to stick around and work on a relationship with him. No more excuses, no more running away.

She wanted to stay in his embrace except she realized she needed to teach a class that evening. Dread began to creep in as she remembered she still didn't figure out how she would talk her students into a full-sized quilt.

CHAPTER 22

Nancy was the most nervous she could remember before teaching a class. She couldn't recall sweaty palms or shaking years ago when she started teaching as a graduate student. She didn't pace or mutter to herself all day. She never watched the clock in dread, unsure of what she would say.

What could she possibly tell her students? She must think of some excuse to convince them to make a full quilt for Janice out of their projects. She sat down at her front register. Her mind tried to comprehend the new knowledge about Gold Street. I don't believe in magic, she started to tell herself, but then felt a breeze and stopped. If she kept thinking like that who knew what kind of bad Joojoo she would stir up?

****

As evening approached her students began to drift in one by one. They slowly started to lay out their quilt squares. Jill returned with the bag of fiber batting samples. When everyone but Aen and Janice arrived, Nancy decided to start the class.

"No Aen?" asked Trish.

"Don't worry ladies," said Raleigh. "She's just running late. Tying up some loose ends from the show. The finale was excellent. Dozens of people came to protest. I held up my sign."

"I bet," said Jill, not unkindly. "Did you go too Bernice?"

"Why I did," replied the shriveled old woman with a big smile. "Raleigh made me a sign as well. You should have seen how uncomfortable a young police officer looked trying to take it away from me."

"Way to go, Bernice," said Keisha.

"What?" asked Ann. She missed the previous week's discussion about Aen's performance. Apparently she was one of the few people in Albuquerque who never saw the evening news broadcasts. She was too busy with Janice's family.

"Never mind, doll," said Raleigh. "We don't need to talk about it anymore. We're here to support you and Janice. How is she?"

Ann's face fell.

"Horrible. Even worse than when I saw you guys last week."

The class gathered around Ann to ask questions.

"What happened?"

"We went through Mike's personal belongings to try sorting everything out. I did forensic audits in the courts for years, so I immediately noticed that the household financial numbers didn't look right. Anyway, Janice never paid much attention to their money. She let her husband handle it all. When we first met, I offered to show her the basics, but she insisted that it was Mike's job."

"Oh, no."

"Oh, yes. I ordered Janice to track down all of their accounts once the death certificate was issued. Turns out he opened an extra bank account and a credit card she never heard of. I ordered the back statements."

Keisha and Trish watched Ann in anticipation for the rest of the story, but everyone else turned away or fidgeted with their projects. They knew this story would end badly.

"Turns out he hid a lover she didn't know about. That's the only explanation for the finances, although now Janice got past the initial shock, she realizes Mike grew distant and critical these past couple years. She blamed herself, menopause symptoms and losing interest in the house, but now she realizes he made her seem like the crazy one."

"Wow, what a truly awful week. How is Janice doing?"

"She's on an emotional roller coaster. One day she's full of rage and the next deeper in grief over the betrayal. I don't know how she will get over this. Not for a very long time. How could he do this to her?"

"I suppose she doesn't want one last conversation with her dead husband anymore?" asked Nancy.

"Well," answered Ann, "I'm not sure it would be the same conversation. She doesn't feel like she owes him an apology anymore for their last fight, but she also will never get the chance to confront him or ask him why he cheated. Every day she thinks of a whole new list of questions about their life together. It's like she'll never get any closure or be able to find peace about her marriage. It kind of haunts her."

"I hope his soul doesn't find any rest either," said Jill.

"Tsk, tsk," said Bernice. "I can't excuse what Mike did, but everyone should be allowed to rest in peace when their time comes."

"Even when they did awful things?" asked Keisha.

"Who among us hasn't made mistakes?" replied Bernice. "I'm not condoning his behavior, but I wish for them both to move on to a better place. Their time with each other should come to an end. That is the way."

Nancy felt a breeze stir. She closed her eyes and tried to ignore it. Soon the wind returned. Okay, okay, she said under her breath.

Nancy rose and addressed her class.

"Ever since Ann told us last week what happened to Janice's husband, I wished we could do something special to comfort her. Yes, we sent flowers and a card, but I mean something unique."

She definitely held the class's attention. She tried to think of some grand excuse to trick the class into making a unified quilt. In the end, she decided on a simple and direct approach.

She took a deep breath. "Instead of each of us sewing our own projects, why don't we combine the squares into one big quilt and give it to Janice to comfort her?"

She exhaled.

The class immediately grew excited. Everyone seemed to like the idea, especially Ann. It would give them something hopeful to work on.

The front door opened, and, as if on cue Aen strolled in. She walked up to the table and unfurled her two large rolls of fabric.

"Look, I got my banners back. An attorney took my case pro-bono. They'll only get pictures of my banners to present in court, not the real things."

The color drained from Ann's face.

"Do we have to use the banners in the quilt?" asked Trish.

"I think they add an exciting touch," said Raleigh.

"Do you still have your fabric paint, Trish?" asked the ever practical Bernice. "We could alter the banners into a more acceptable design. Something a bit more comforting."

"They could be rockets," said Keisha, getting into the spirit.

"Umm, not very comforting," commented Raleigh.

"What about mushrooms?" suggested Jill. "We can completely cover some of them and make the rest into colorful toadstools, and add flowers and butterflies. It could be quite fanciful."

Nancy worried how Aen would react, but once the class explained the quilt, she said it was trippy like a medicine sand painting for Janice. She was fine with her banners being altered that way.

Soon the class laid out all their squares of fabric into one large quilt design. Obviously they couldn't all piece it together at the same time. Nancy managed to find a couple of sewing machines in the back room. She figured out a sewing schedule for people to take turns during the week, and then they could be ready for top stitching by hand by the last class. Nancy would set it up on a frame for a quilting bee.

****

The next day Fay stopped by the quilt shop.

"You didn't bring me any tea," remarked Nancy. She didn't mean to sound pushy or ungrateful, but she sure could use the relaxation.

"Didn't you know your magic only works in your own store? Perhaps I forgot to mention that part."

Nancy mulled it over. No wonder Fay always offered her soda water, wine or lemonade at her own house.

"How are things going with Bob?" Fay tried to sound casual.

"Wonderful," gushed Nancy. They talked and emailed constantly since their lunch. She was excited a whole new chapter was opening in her life until she stopped to look Fay directly in the eyes. Fay tried to collect her composure. She would always be polite. A sense of tenderness shot through Nancy. She never thought about how getting involved with Bob affected Fay.

"I owe you big thanks for sending Bob to my house the other day."

"It's worthwhile to see you both happy."

Fay displayed a faraway look Nancy couldn't read. Sadness seemed to cross her face. Just as quickly, Fay straightened up with a stiff upper lip.

Nancy walked over to Fay and wrapped her in a tight hug. "Really, I owe you a lot."

Fay relaxed and a smile stole across her face. "I do enjoy seeing the two of you together. Bob looks like he just won the lottery."

Nancy blushed as she took a step back from Fay. "You're okay seeing us together?"

"Bob is quite a catch. I won't deny it. Seeing you two lovebirds reminds me how long it's been since I did any courting. I think I'm getting too old for such things. Plus, every year seems like there are fewer and fewer eligible men."

"Fay, you still look wonderful. Any man would be lucky to be with you. Are you going to join the dating service?"

"Those young folks are trying to talk me into it. I don't know. Maybe it's time to take that trip to visit my friend Bunny in Florida."

"Not that again!"

"You would be fine without me. You made a bunch of friends on Gold Street and now you're starting to see Bob."

"But who would serve your special tea?"

"Dear, that's the question I just can't answer. I wonder about it myself."

"You told me not to walk away from my special gift. You said it yourself," Nancy pouted. "Speaking of special gifts--how is the quilt going?"

"I actually think we'll be able to do this. I can't believe I'm listening to you and Jane."

"You'll thank me."

"What if Jane is wrong about my abilities? How do I even know this is going to work? How did you figure out about your gift?"

"Well," answered Fay thoughtfully, "it started when Jane and I talked about my first day at the tea shop and gallery. I sat at the front table and remembered the tea parties I gave for my dolls and how much comfort I could serve. Jane told me a happy memory was a good starting point to figuring out my gifts."

"Oh," said Nancy, "that reminds me of my first day. I looked at Jane's computer through the travel company window and saw my old quilt. I immediately was reminded of my circle of girlfriends from almost forty years ago and our fantastic quilting bees. That's when I knew I needed to open my quilt shop on Gold Street..."

Fay gave her a knowing look.

Nancy imagined somewhere Jane smiled triumphantly.

CHAPTER 23

The following Monday Bob didn't arrive until mid-morning, allowing Nancy to sleep in. He rode up to her house on his shiny red bicycle, which he would later admit he bought just for the occasion, with fancy panniers neatly packed on the back for lunch.

They decided to take off slow. They headed in the direction of the river at an easy coast downhill until they rode among the highrises of Downtown's business district. They made their way to a coffee shop on the western edge called Java Joe's. The place was packed with customers listening to live music. It exuded a Downtown funky feel, painted in bright colors with local art hanging on the walls and bars on the windows. This area of old Route 66 was still a bit dicey. Across the street sat a partially burned, abandoned hotel. Bob told her it was used in the film No Country for Old Men.

Beyond the hotel was a park frequented by homeless and drug dealers. Further down Central Avenue were motels frequented by down-on-their-luck people in need of low hourly rates.

Still, Java Joe's roasted their own coffee and made surprisingly good Belgian waffles with freshly whipped whole cream topping. Nancy figured she could cycle off the extra calories.

A fascinating cross-section of customers came in. Some appeared to be artists and musicians, while others wore business clothing. A young couple minded a group of children. An entire clan of skinny, hardcore cyclists walked in together in coordinating yellow and black spandex outfits. She guessed they were retired. She marveled a crowd of mature people could all be so fit. Their high-end bikes sat stacked in rows, locked together on the parking lot fence. They seemed to move together as a single organism.

Nancy never tired of reading all the different flyers posted in Java Joe's windows, typical of local coffee shops, which formed a sort of community bulletin board. In the next couple weeks she could see local bands, watch an indie film, go to a yoga retreat, join a protest, or get her Chakras realigned.

They lingered at the coffee shop to enjoy the leisurely pace. They began to get past basic questions about each other, such as where they grew up or their favorites classes in college. She felt a nagging concern in the back of her mind about whether they became physically involved too quickly. But, with each passing hour of conversation, she began to realize they shared lust with the potential to turn into a deep friendship.

Would they fall in love?

She decided to take a deep breath and just relax for the day. For once she was determined to appreciate what was in front of her instead of becoming lost in regrets about the past and concerns about the future.

When they finished their coffee, they cycled through some of the neighborhoods, past bungalows and low square stucco apartment buildings centered on grassy courtyards. The housing somehow reminded her of some of the bungalows she saw while visiting California. The view changed when they reached Fay's neighborhood. They shared insights about varieties of houses. He explained that the neighborhood, Huning Castle, was mostly marsh until river flood control was enacted. Unlike the rest of Downtown, this neighborhood wouldn't be built until around the Second World War. The wide lawns, abundant trees, winding roads and various types of ranch houses produced the feel of a suburb.

They turned down Laguna Boulevard. She decided it was her favorite street in Albuquerque. It felt like a boulevard in a European city, with towering cottonwood trees. They rode past the private country club to Tingley Beach.

At one time the Tingley ponds were actually used as summer beach recreation. The water brought welcome relief in the desert before air conditioning. But, like many public swimming facilities in the 1950s, the water closed to the public. Despite a few avid fishers, the area declined into near abandonment. In recent times the city revived the ponds into well-loved stocked fishing ponds.

They stopped at the ponds to watch the flocks of birds. Canadian geese paced in preparation for their long northward migration ahead. Several Sandhill Cranes passed overhead. Ducks quacked noisily, and stomped and chased in preparation for their spring mating season. Bob pointed out a pair of mallards as they flew towards water in the arroyo next to the road.

They were gifted with mild winter weather in the mid 60's for the day. Nancy appreciated the sunshine on her back as they rode.

Next Bob took her to the bike trail along the bosque. Nancy tried peering through the trees to find the Rio Grande, but they weren't close enough yet to the river.

They first headed south on the bike trail past the zoo. The roar of a lion mixed with the sound of chattering monkeys. He slowed so they could watch a zookeeper throw bales of hay in the elephant pen. Next they made their way along the winding tree-lined path until they crossed under a bridge. When they reached the other side, he pointed out the National Hispanic Cultural Center. Impressive massive walls stood in contrast to a stark, yet beautiful, plaza.

On the trail beyond the center were ugly industrial areas littered with discarded parts. Luckily they didn't ride long until they reached the agricultural fields of the South Valley.

Bob pulled aside from the trail to rest on a bench. They watched a tractor till one of the fields while a small group of workers walked in a line to plant another.

She was content to sit for a while watching water flow in the irrigation ditches. She needed to get to the bosque more often. She still wasn't adjusted to the dryness of the desert.

When she was ready, which took longer than she cared to admit, they ventured south until they reached a set of picnic tables near a road overpass at Rio Bravo. They walked their bikes along gravel paths until they reached a choice picnic table in the sun.

By now their bodies began to fall into a rhythm together. No words were needed. He gently unpacked the bags on his bike. He surprised her with a traditional red and white checkered table cloth with napkins to match. Next he pulled out a couple of hand-brewed root beers which were still cold. He reached around until he found a bowl of grapes and a large bag of BBQ flavored potato chips.

She raised her eyebrows at the last selection but he insisted no picnic was complete without the chips.

The sandwiches proved to be a delight. He paired thick slices of ham with broiled slices of pears topped with Brie cheese, and seasoned with fine mustard on crusty baguettes. He said he noticed the sandwich on the day they visited Café Lush.

The bread alone would satisfy her. She greedily tore into the soft bread beyond the tasty hard crust. She allowed the soft Brie to melt in her mouth.

Somewhat stuffed, she assumed the bike panniers were empty. She was pleasantly surprised when, after a rest, he lifted out a sturdy box.

He mumbled something about not being sure the pastries survived the trip. When he opened the box and dug through the tissue, two perfect cream balls from Flying Star Café emerged. One was covered in lush dark chocolate while the other was drizzled with rich caramel and sea salt.

"Here's the dilemma," he said. "I don't know which one was better."

"I have an idea..."

She picked up the caramel one to gently nip the end. Wonderful sweetness was followed by a hint of salt. She then slowly inserted her tongue into the hole to bring a small amount of cream to her lips. She slowly slurped the cream with her tongue.

Nancy vowed before the bike trip that she would pretend they were sweet innocent school kids out on a harmless date, but she found in Bob's presence that she enjoyed her sensuality as a mature woman. If she really remembered what it was like to be a teenager, she was gangly and awkward. She realized that while he made her feel young again in certain ways, she also appreciated that they could be comfortable with who they had become in life. They didn't need to play games. They could appreciate each other for who they really were. Bob didn't want her to pretend or act. He genuinely liked her for herself.

Bob looked entranced as she slowly moved her tongue across her lips to remove the last of the cream.

"Here, now you take a bite."

He slowly bit and sucked.

They somehow managed to pass the small cream puff back and forth a couple times before finishing it.

"I have a different idea for the other one."

She sat down directly beside him on the bench. She held up the chocolate cream puff for him to take a bite, and then she nipped a piece, and left the pastry in her lips. She bent over and kissed him deeply with the pastry. Creaminess moved from mouth to mouth.

His face appeared almost pained.

"Okay, enough of this," he said as he jumped up from the table. "It's our first official day of dating. I'm not that kind of a guy."

He wore a big grin. He clearly was.

They finished and packed up the remains of the picnic lunch. He locked up the bikes.

"Why don't I show you river vegetation? This is part of what I studied in the last couple years."

He led her down the winding path through a stand of trees and long plant stems. They reached the river's edge. For the next couple of hours he explained the river's flow. He showed her different types of plants—which were native and which were invasives threatening the ecosystem. She knew she would never remember all of the various names he seemed to remember with ease.

He pointed out different types of animal tracks, varieties of birds, and a tree in the process of being gnawed down by beavers living on the river. They located a couple stumps nearby where the beavers were already successful in their endless construction activities.

He showed her man-made bat houses nailed to the trees and explained the difference from a bird house. He promised sometime later in the year, when the weather was warmer, he would take her to watch bats fly out from under the bridge at the I-40 freeway overpass at sunset.

She didn't question they would still spend time together.

As he continued to talk, she lost herself in the sound of his voice. It was starting to become familiar. His words were always somehow soothing.

They eventually made their way to their locked bikes and headed back north on the bike trail toward the tall buildings of Downtown. The afternoon sunlight started to sink between the trees. She felt a certain twinge of sadness to know the day would come to an end. Couldn't they live forever in a single perfect day like this?

He graciously stopped a couple times at benches along the bike trail with the pretense of pointing out some sort of plant. Really, he was making sure she wouldn't get too tired. She definitely sat too much at her store.

The day felt like a vacation. It was strange to roll back into the main area of Downtown and see business people walk around in suits. He suggested they stop for what the French call gouter—a late afternoon snack.

What better place than P'tit Louis, a picturesque little bistro which prided itself on taking customers back to 1920s Paris? They excelled at cooking French classics. After locking their bicycles to a light pole, they wandered into the mostly empty tiny restaurant. They settled on champagne with Les Escargots de Bourgogne and a sample of cheese. Nancy admired the architectural details—a wooden bar with a large picture mirror behind, a few tables with starched white linens, black and white photos, and a floor of small white hexagonal tile to match the historic lobby of the Sunshine office building nearby. She lost herself in the bubbles of champagne as old French songs played in the bistro.

She found the gouter refreshing, which was helpful since they still needed to cycle up the hill from the center of Downtown to her house in EDo. Luckily, she didn't live at the far end of the neighborhood where the climb was steepest.

Driving around the city in a car, it was easy to forget the city was built on the steep sides of a valley. However, on a bicycle the incline became obvious. She was glad most of Downtown and the valley was mercifully flat. The day's ride was not strenuous.

When they arrived at her house they both lounged on her couch and nodded off for a short nap. Upon waking Nancy felt the inclination to be intimate, but Bob resisted. He insisted the day was not done yet.

They walked to the Hotel Parq Central, a hospital built in the 1920s to serve, like several others as part of the sanatorium movement, a growing population of TB patients who flocked to Sun City in hopes of improved health. Albuquerque's spa cures status faded as cures for tuberculosis were found in the 1940s and 50s. Bob explained the building housed a mental hospital for a time. Recently it was renovated into a hotel.

In the summer the outdoor areas were beautifully landscaped with gardens. They decided to head up to the Apothecary rooftop lounge to watch the end of the day. They settled on the patio near a heater to marvel at one of the best views in town. Bob explained that the mountain was named Sandia after the Spanish word for watermelon. The east side is green with trees. The west side facing town turns red at sunset like a watermelon. As if on cue, with the fading light, the mountains obliged with red hues. They watched as the city lights began to turn on one by one. To the west they could still barely see the outline of volcanoes on the west mesa.

For the first time that day they sat mostly in silence absorbed by breath-taking views and changing patterns of color. The bar specialized in cocktails from the Prohibition era. She was tempted to try a mix with Aztec chocolate bitters, but decided to stick to a champagne cocktail.

Once it was fully dark and their cocktails settled, they decided to walk to the Artichoke Café for dinner. Bob insisted on treating her to a nicer meal. He knew while sales in her store were starting to improve, she was in no position to go dutch. She was still on a budget.

Luckily, they were able to get a table. Often people without a reservation could only sit at the bar or were turned away. They sat at the front by a picture window facing the street.

"This is a great spot to watch folks walk by on the street," remarked Bob.

"Oh, my."

"What?"

Nancy developed an unusual expression on her face. "I remember seeing you before I met you."

"At your fabric store when I tried to pick out a green color? I'm glad I won't need to do that again by myself. I was totally lost," said Bob. He took her hand. "I'm lost in a lot of ways without you, Nan."

She still thought about seeing him earlier. "This is so wonderful. Before I met you Fay and I ate dinner down the street at the Standard Diner. We saw you walk by. Fay knew she met you before, but couldn't place where."

Her face turned a bit red. "We both wanted to get to know you better. Do you believe in love at first sight? I think I knew you were right for me before even meeting you."

"I believe in it now." He smiled.

"I suppose it's none of my business, but I wonder where you were going? Now I recall that I was jealous that you might meet someone here and I didn't know if you were married or not."

He tried to remember as she calculated the day for him. Nothing stood out in his memory. "Sorry, I can't recall. I don't think it was a date, unless we headed to the pizza place."

"Never mind. The important part is that I knew I wanted to be here with you. I even wished we would go someplace romantic like the Artichoke Café together."

"I'm glad you didn't give up on me."

Nancy grinned.

They enjoyed sharing an appetizer of roasted garlic baguette with Montrachet goat cheese, roasted red peppers, and olives. They sipped Pinot Noir wine.

As they nibbled, Bob explained about the cheese. "A true Montrachet comes from the Burgundy region of France. It's rolled into a log shape, covered with salted ash, and then aged wrapped in vine or chestnut leaves."

"Is it aged for a long time?"

"Oh, no. It's a fresh milk cheese. Notice how soft and creamy it is? Once it starts to age too much it will get somewhat bitter and watery."

Nancy savored every bite of creaminess.

"You know," she said, "maybe we're taking this first date thing too far. All of this sensuous food and drink is really putting me in the mood for intimacies."

"You are so tempting—but no. You are the most special thing to come into my life in a very long time. I'm still sorry we got involved so quickly. I really wish we did this first. I'm not about to make the same mistake twice."

"You don't care to, um, get physical for a long time? How long did you want to wait?"

"I want to wait until we're ready for a serious relationship."

"Serious?" She felt panic begin to rise from deep inside her. Her legs started to twitch and she felt the urge to excuse herself to the ladies room.

Bob grabbed her hand, as if sensing that she was ready to flee.

"We don't need to talk about this tonight. I said I wouldn't push. I tell you what. I won't bring up the subject again. You tell me when you're ready to discuss our future together."

"Are you implying we should get married or something?"

"A piece of paper doesn't make a relationship, I know that for sure. I'm ready to find someone who wants to work on being together every day. I wouldn't mind tying the knot again if we thought it would help. What's most important is someone who is willing to commit to a relationship together."

Nancy gulped the last of her wine. She tried to think of conversation but nothing came to mind. Bob started to stroke her hand in a soothing way. His veterinary training seemed to let him sense when someone was in need of calming. He made no demands. He simply waited until she found her composure again.

Nancy's dinner was hand-made pumpkin ravioli with butternut squash-spinach-ricotta filling, sage beurre blanc, which Bob explained was a white wine butter sauce, roasted tomatoes and toasted hazelnuts. She drank another glass of Pinot while he chose a Malbec.

Bob ate grilled beef tenderloin with pommes Anna, asparagus, a shallot-blue cheese butter and sherry demi glaze. He shared fascinating details about the potato dish, which was often cooked in a special double baking dish of copper from France called la cocotte a pommes Anna. He used two spoons to demonstrate how the top half and lower half fit together during cooking. The dish would need to be inverted every ten minutes so both sides would develop a crispy and golden crust.

Perhaps they drank enough wine.

They decided on coffee to accompany their shared dessert of apple bread pudding—crème fraiche ice cream, apple chips, apple caramel, and apple gelee with toasted hazelnuts. Nancy tried to decide if she liked the apple desert better than the brie with apple compote down the street at the diner, but she couldn't make a choice. So many things in the neighborhood were so wonderful.

"You know," she said, "I don't think I can leave Downtown anymore."

"That's why they call New Mexico 'The Land of Entrapment'. People check in, but they don't check out."

"I thought it was the 'Land of Enchantment'."

"Do you know how many residents planned to drive to California but ended up here because this is where they ran out of gas? Literally?"

"Guess that's as good a reason as any. I mean, we make all these plans, but then life happens anyway. That should be the state's new slogan—A Great Place to Run Out of Gas."

They both giggled. They definitely drank enough wine.

While walking back to Nancy's house, they didn't feel the winter evening cold which settled in. Despite her wine buzz, Nancy started to plan her quilting bee. Would it be a success? Did she remember accurately how much time was involved? She began to work out the details in her head. Bob didn't seem to mind her preoccupation. He left her at her front door with a simple kiss.

CHAPTER 24

Nancy decided to make her last class, the quilting bee, into a party. She planned an array of food and drink. Everyone would bring extra people. With enough help, and a very simple stitched design, they should be able to almost finish the quilt in a long day.

Nancy's first helpers showed up when she opened her store in the morning. Small groups continued to sit and work at the quilting frame throughout the day. They all agreed everyone should be present for the last couple hours of quilting in the evening to celebrate.

By nightfall, Fay arrived with surprise pizzas, absolutely delicious deserts, and plenty more drinks. Keisha brought Theresa M and a couple of their friends, bearing even more food.

Raleigh made a half-hearted attempt to learn to stitch by hand, and then set about as host. He refreshed plates of food, refilled glasses, and walked around with expensive hand cream to massage tired fingers. Nancy was free to concentrate on sewing.

Aen arrived with musician friends. Nancy worried about what Aen might consider appropriate sewing music. Everyone was pleased when they turned out to be from the Church of Beethoven on Fifth Street. The musicians stuck mainly to upbeat classical music and improvised jazz. They performed publically on Sunday mornings. Nancy made a note to herself she and Bob should hear them.

Aen sat down next to Keisha and Theresa M. Soon they talked about Aen's job at Starbucks. Theresa M mentioned she might search for a barista soon to assist at the Jumping Bean Café. She thought about holding open mic nights, literary readings, and poetry slams. She wanted to grow her business beyond people who wandered in for coffee in the morning.

Jill and Trish both brought their kids. The children ran circles and hid below the quilt frame until Raleigh took both of them on his lap and proceeded to tell them amazing fairy tales. He remarked fairies were a specialty. Nancy watched and wondered if he ever wished he became a father.

Bernice brought the daughter she lived with, a woman just a little older than Nancy. The companionship between the two was amazing. They talked about their recent travels abroad and an upcoming art exhibit for Bernice in Los Angeles. Nancy didn't know Bernice showed her work on both coasts.

The quilter who most surprised Nancy was Bob. As much as she enjoyed his company and appreciated his support, she questioned his ability to sew. Unjustly, as it turned out. Years of stitching up pets made him one of the most competent quilters in the room. He amazed everyone by bringing along surgical supplies: cutters, thin half-circle needles and needle holders, similar to pliers. He taught several people how to use them quickly to pick up the pace of the sewing. He gave away all the needles he brought with him so some of the quilters could try them at home. The thick rounded needles were particularly helpful for sewing fabrics like upholstery, leather and denim, or repairing torn items like couches.

Ann arrived last. Janice considered coming, but still couldn't face a crowd of well-wishers. Instead, Ann brought hers and Janice's teenage daughters. Their sons decided to stay home with Janice and play video games. The three teenage girls surveyed the situation unhappily, and then sat down on the end near Keisha. For a while they appeared lost and spent more time texting than trying to learn to sew. Finally Keisha engaged them talking about boys and clothes. Keisha gave them some style tips about the upcoming fashion season. Theresa M gave suggestions about finding cheap vintage jewelry.

Nancy worried the night would be too solemn. Instead, people laughed as the music kept tempo. New friendships were made, and the quilt was complete, stitched entirely by hand. Nancy unrolled the frame bars and took off the quilt for everyone to see.

Applause filled the room.

In the center was a photo of a dancer taken by Bernice. Trish took it home and hand-painted it in bright shades of red, combining their skills. Trish also added on beads and tokens representing strength.

The rest of the squares were mismatches of various colors and designs: more photos from Bernice, traditional quilt patterns from Ann, Janice and Nancy, Keisha's bold abstract designs from the recycled bag of clothes, plain wool fabric squares in the four corners from Jill, and a couple of Raleigh's ironed together squares in shades of white. Aen's two repainted banners ran down the sides. The batting came from Jill's bag of fiber samples, unfortunately of different densities pieced together haphazardly.

Nancy held the quilt up high. All in all, she thought, it was one of the ugliest and most misshapen quilts she ever saw, and it was absolutely wonderful. Each lopsided square, each uneven stitch, each clump of bunched batting was done in love.

The group gave a cheer and everyone hugged. Nancy folded the quilt away carefully. She would spend the next couple weeks adding binding around the edges to finish the quilt.

The party slowly wound down. Nancy took Ann aside to try to figure out how to get Janice to come by the quilt store to invoke its powers.

"How is Janice doing?"

"She just doesn't know what to think anymore. She is so consumed by Mike's affair she can't focus on anything else. I know it's really soon after his death, but I worry about her finding something to move forward in life. She knows her kids will soon leave home."

"Do you think she still wishes she could see Mike one more time?"

"I asked her. She got real thoughtful, but she didn't have an answer."

"Would you ask her again?"

Ann looked at Nancy in surprise.

"Let's give her the quilt when she's ready to talk to Mike."

Okay, that was lame, thought Nancy to herself. Ann appeared to think she lost all of her marbles.

"Ah, you know," said Nancy, "let's get Janice to take comfort in the quilt and talk through her issues with Mike. Maybe it would help her start to move on. It would be like a quilt intervention. We could use picking up the quilt as the excuse for her to come here and talk. Can you get her to come to the store? That is, when she seems ready?"

"Okay," answered Ann reluctantly. She didn't seem to follow Nancy's logic, but was too worn out to argue the wisdom of such an enterprise. "I'll call you when Janice seems ready."

****

Some time passed before Nancy got the call from Ann.

"Janice seems to be doing a little bit better. Some days okay, some days not so."

"I've heard it goes in cycles."

"She's starting to come to terms with her life. She'll receive income to compensate for the loss of Mike plus payments from insurance, survivor benefits and whatnot. Luckily money isn't an issue. The kids are settled back in school and she's done sorting through Mike's things. Using her organizational skills kept her busy for a while."

"And now?"

"She's starting to think about the affair again. About the big fight with Mike on the day he was killed."

"Do you think she's ready for the, um, therapeutic intervention we talked about? You could bring her in the evening after my business hours."

"Anything that might help her I would like to try. She has too much time on her hands right now with no direction. Just this week I asked her to sort through and organize one of my client's paperwork. Their filing cabinet was a disaster area. They were amazed she got everything in top shape in less than an afternoon. They tried to set up a system for years. Janice seemed to intuitively know what would work for them."

"Before Mike was killed she stopped by the store. She did wonders in arranging my sewing notions."

"Keep Janice in mind if you know of anyone in need of home organizing."

After Ann hung up, Nancy sat contemplating how to set up the evening for Janice. She wasn't entirely convinced the magic thing would even work. Jane and Fay didn't mention any rules or special preparation.

In any case, Nancy looked forward to Janice finally getting her quilt. Everyone asked her to take photos to post on the website. She already blogged about the quilting bee and how much fun it was. She already received inquiries about how others could set up quilting bee parties like hers.

CHAPTER 25

A couple nights later Fay assisted Nancy in a cleanup of the store in anticipation of Janice's big night.

"Don't think I'm nitpicking, dear, but the sad little plastic cupid in your front display window absolutely needs to go. Is he now the Easter Cherub?"

The spring winds came to New Mexico. Fay explained it happened every year with the changing seasons. She should be careful about the seedlings on her front porch.

"But the porch is screened in."

"You don't understand how strong these winds will get."

Still, Nancy basked in the blue skies and warm sun. She felt delight in the fruit trees' burst of blooms. She awoke happily in the mornings to the birds chirping outside her bedroom window.

Fay cleared her throat to bring back Nancy's attention.

"I am telling you this as a friend--your window display is horrid. Why didn't you change it?"

"Because I can't decorate like you. There, I said it."

The two women stared at each other. Neither one brought up the subject of their big fight, when Fay took her tree and decorations out of the quilt shop window.

"I have an Easter tree," said Fay.

Both women started to laugh.

"Okay, not really. But please, won't you let me do something?"

Fay raided her own store and came back with two large boxes of goodies. She suggested a spring tea party display with loads of beautiful draped fabrics. At the table, in the place of cookies, would be small swatches of expensive fabrics Nancy just received in shipments.

"Can cupid sit at the table?"

"No, because he is going to a happier place. I'm going to burn him."

They talked about Nancy making small quilt samples for her future summer window display. Fay thought of laying them out like a blanket for a picnic. She could already picture a perfect basket and dishes adorned with fabric swatches folded like napkins. She could even try making folded cloth animals, like cruise ships use for their towels.

Fay and Nancy had just finished assembling the fabric tea party when Ann arrived with Janice. After awkward pleasantries were exchanged, Nancy led them over to her table.

"We were thinking," began Nancy, "that the quilt class would like to give you a present."

"My daughters told me about the quilt. That's really sweet of everyone. They had a really good time at the party." Janice added, "I hope they remembered to say thank you."

She seemed to stall. Nancy knew that Ann had told her about the basic idea. They wanted her to wrap up in the quilt and start an "imaginary" conversation with her dead husband.

"Go get the quilt," said Fay, taking control. She rummaged in her purse. "I know I have my camera in here somewhere."

Taking pictures of Janice with her new quilt helped ease her into the main event.

"Do you feel like you are ready to do this?" asked Ann.

"No," said Janice honestly. "I'll never be ready."

"But this will help," said a voice from behind Nancy. She almost jumped out of her skin.

"Jesus, Jane! You do that to me all the time. Must you sneak up on people?" Nancy's nerves were clearly almost as frayed as Janice's. "This is my whacky neighbor Jane, who owns the Cosmic Travel & Tour Co."

Fay gave Nancy an admonishing look.

"I heard what happened," Jane said gently to Janice, ignoring Nancy's last comment. "Please let us help."

Jane draped the quilt around Janice's shoulders and told her to sit at the end of the table, then motioned the others to back away.

Jane gave directions softly. "Janice, I want you to close your eyes and hug the quilt tightly. Feel all the loving energy coming from everyone who stitched it together for you. Relax and concentrate."

"On what?"

"I want you to picture your husband the last time you saw him. What was he wearing? What was the expression on his face?"

Janice winced.

"Keep going. I feel the call getting stronger. I want you to keep focusing and imagine him at the other end of the table."

A strong gust of wind came through the store and the electricity flickered out. Enough light still shone through the front window Fay was able to find candles in her boxes and matches. She lit the candles and placed them in the middle of the table.

"Oh, springtime in Albuquerque," chattered Nancy nervously.

"Shh," said Jane. She continued, "Okay, Janice, I want you to focus a little harder. I want you to picture reaching out your hand to Mike. I want you to actually welcome him into the room."

"That's really hard," said Janice.

"I know sweetheart, but you can do it. Keep concentrating. I want you to picture him reaching out his hand to meet yours. He is wearing his wedding ring. What does his hand look like? Can you picture it?"

"Yes."

Nancy let her mind wander to her ex-husband. She could suddenly see his hands perfectly, with a thin band of gold still on his finger.

She first noticed his hands while they were both in graduate school. She was attracted to the way his slender fingers could gracefully hold a pencil. He was a pure academic immersed in his studies, his nose always poked into a book, ready to discuss some theory. People naturally flocked to him to hear his ideas.

A smile came to Nancy's lips. How many years was it since Nancy remembered that? Since she thought any kind of gentle thoughts about her marriage? It was good to reminisce about the early happy times.

She could picture fall in the Midwest, when the air started to turn cold and the trees burst with brightly colored leaves. Students gathered on campus full of youthful energy and bright dreams. She, her future husband, and their friends—all of them would change the world. Political discussion could last an entire night. Nancy was sure she would change how people thought about different cultures and traditions. She would leave an impact.

It was a time in her life when she thought everything seemed possible.

She tried to hold on to the memory of what it felt like to be so young and optimistic. She let her mind drift for a while until she heard Jane's voice again.

"You're doing very good Janice. I feel Mike's presence getting closer. Now I want you to focus on your two hands touching. I want you to think so hard you can actually feel his skin. Do you remember what that felt like?"

"It's hard. I already forgot so much about him."

"Now you'll remember. Stay focused for me. Don't get distracted. I want you, in your mind's eye, to see his hand wrapping around your hand. Can you feel it? Feel the warmth from his skin. And the touch. He is grabbing hold of your fingers. He is holding on tightly."

Ann let out a shriek.

There, sitting at the other end of the table in the candlelight, was Mike. A soft image of him which glowed slightly.

Ann began to shake. Strangely, Janice sat calmly at the table. She searched every inch of his body, trying to commit it to long term memory.

"Ann, dear, let's get you next door. You were under entirely too much stress lately and are in need of a cup of tea," said Fay.

Fay wrapped her arm around Ann, who started to shake and chatter so loudly it sounded like her teeth were about to come out of her head. Fay would later tell her she fainted in the quilt store from exhaustion. They would leave it up to Janice whether she wanted to try to explain to her friend what really happened.

Nancy started to follow behind the two women to go to the tea shop when Jane stopped her.

"This is your miracle. You might as well stick around to see it."

Yes, thought Nancy, this is my magic. Until now she was unwilling to believe the quilt would work. She watched as Janice huddled under their handiwork. Some of the stitching was neat and tight while others sewed large, sloppy rows. The different types of fabric reflected the candle light in a multitude of ways, as if each of the quilters left marks of their own personalities to shine from the cloth.

Nancy suddenly understood the quilt was a mosaic of life downtown, shaped by the wide range of people who congregated within the buildings each day. Everyone added their own unique piece to create a messy, disorderly, misshapen but wonderful whole.

Nancy and Jane continued to wait patiently for Janice to collect her thoughts.

Janice sucked in her breath, in preparation to speak to her husband.

"When you first died Mike, I would have done anything to talk with you again. Absolutely anything. I would have sold my soul to the devil if that's what it took, because I thought I owed you an apology. Can you believe that?"

Anger rose in her voice.

"I don't owe you anything!"

The misty figure of her dead husband did not move or even show expression. She would later tell Nancy he remained just as she last remembered seeing him, at the breakfast table on the morning of his accident.

"How I wanted to see you again... until I found out about your affair. Do you know what I thought then?"

Nancy wondered if Janice was about to become hysterical. Not that she would blame the poor woman.

"I wondered how you could do that to me! For a moment, I was even glad you were dead. It serves you right."

Nancy wondered if it was possible to hurt a ghost's feelings.

The apparition didn't answer out loud. He didn't seem to own a voice. Instead, each of the women in the room could hear his thoughts inside their own heads.

I'm sorry.

"Sorry? Do you know how you tormented me? How badly you treated me? How you acted like I was the one not committed to our marriage? When all of this time you knew you were cheating? Were you planning to leave me?"

No, I always loved you. I wish I could be with you now.

"Can a ghost cheat and lie?" asked Nancy out loud, despite herself.

"He can't cheat—he's dead. No more marriage contract," answered Jane. "Now, shush."

Nancy still wondered if ghosts can lie.

"I wanted this for so long but never thought it would happen," said Janice. "Now I don't really know what to say. I rehearsed my words to pretend to have a conversation with you a hundred different ways. But after learning about your affair, I can hardly stand to see you. Please forgive me."

"Why?"

We both need peace.

"Are you going to visit your lover, too?"

No, it was already over.

Ann would later confirm the mysterious charges on the hidden credit card stopped three months before Mike died. As near as Ann could piece together by searching through old cell phone records and his hidden email account, they had stopped all contact by then. Ann offered to show Janice, but she decided to tell Ann to delete and shred everything instead.

"Was she more beautiful than me? A better lover? Just more fun to be around?"

No, stop. You never did anything wrong.

"Why? I don't understand."

Nancy cringed at the raw pain Janice must feel.

It was me. I was feeling old. She looked like you did when I first met you, with long hair down her back. Just like you years ago. And she laughed, the way we used to laugh together.

"It's been a long time since we laughed together."

On the day I crashed we had that big fight.

"I felt so guilty. Like maybe I caused you to not pay attention. Like I was the one responsible for your death because I distracted you."

Nancy could hear Janice choke back her sobs.

Leaving the house that morning I decided it was time to come clean about the affair. I knew I was wrecking our lives. We fought constantly. I just didn't want to grow up and accept responsibility for what I did to you, but the fantasy I could go back in time thirty years was over. It was time to stop blaming you.

"Were you thinking about me when you died?"

Sorry, babe. It was an extra-large Ruben sandwich. My favorite with extra salty sauerkraut.

That must be some type of inside joke because Janice started to laugh softly. Nancy hoped Janice started to find some sort of resolution.

You have to let me go now.

"I don't want to."

They all noticed the image of Mike began to fade.

"No, please stay longer. We can sit and visit. I want to tell you what the kids are doing. I'm not ready for you to go.'

Be strong for the kids. Babe, let go.

"No, we have more to discuss. I have so many questions for you. I should have written them down."

The image at the end of the table was reduced to a flicker.

"Wait, no, it's not time to go."

Softly, in the distance — I love you.

"I love you, too. Please say something more."

Janice was met with only silence. The image was gone. She shivered under her quilt.

She turned to the two women behind her. "When can I call him back? We're not done. It can't be over."

"He's gone, I can feel it," said Jane quietly. "I'm sorry. It's time to release him in your heart. He can't come back here anymore. I sense the quilt only works once."

Janice didn't seem to know how to react. Nancy began to wonder what she must be feeling.

Was she happy her wish was granted?

Still angry?

Ready to forgive?

Or torn in half at seeing him again?

Nancy and Jane stepped forward to embrace Janice, who remained wrapped up in the quilt.

"How are you doing?" asked Jane softly.

Janice closed her eyes and took a while before answering. She gently swayed as she replayed the scene in her mind. Suddenly she sat up straighter in the chair and turned to the others. "I couldn't do this again. It's too much! Don't get me wrong. I really wanted to see Mike, but..."

"But what?"

"It's really too weird. Those pants and shirts he was wearing? I already donated them to the thrift store."

"Yes, sweetheart," said Jane, "He's already gone. Time must move forward."

Janice abruptly changed her mind. She was on an emotional roller coaster. "But there are so many things I still want to talk to him about. I have his wedding ring in my jewelry box. I can't sort out whether he would want me to keep it. My friend suggested melting our rings down together to make small pendants for the children." Janice turned to look Jane directly in the eyes. "Will it make him mad?"

Nobody answered.

Nancy started to rub Janice's back.

"He's really gone," said Jane. "We can't ask him any more questions."

"I guess I'm now going to make plans for the future by myself," said Janice. She looked despondent. "I'm exhausted."

"He is going to where he is meant to be," said Jane.

A quiet fell over the room again.

"Goodbye," whispered Janice softly.

****

Bob was waiting for Nancy when she locked up her store for the night. She was exhausted and couldn't begin to find the words to describe her evening at the store. However, she did feel at peace. Finally, she knew she'd made the right decision to move to Albuquerque to open a quilt shop. She'd found a way to stitch together a new life. Silently they climbed onto their bicycles together to make the journey home.

About Samantha Clark

Samantha Clark channels her background in commercial real estate and business coaching into the fictional characters of Gold Street. Her love of textiles started as a young child. Growing up in Northeast Ohio her great-grandmother taught her how to quilt when she was five. She would go on to study clothing design at Pratt Institute while working in textile restoration in New York City. She continues to hand sew textile art. Someday, like her character Bernice (named in honor of her great-grandmother), she would like to learn how to combine photography and sewing.

Follow Samantha's projects on Facebook at Mariposa.Notes

Recent Releases by Casa de Snapdragon

A Dance in the Woods: A Mother's Insight
Janet K. Brennan
ISBN: 978-1-937240-48-6
Genre: Memoirs
Available in paperback and eBook

Brennan has created the most remarkable work of art, the wonder-work of a genius. It is a complete revelation of an intensely individual apprehension of death. A Dance in the Woods, in essence, is the author Brennan herself, as she tries to find a way to recover from the trauma of her daughter death, and her burning passion searches some sign of her resurrection so that she might find peace of mind.

-- Dr. Santosh Kumar, Dean of English Department, A.D. College, Allahabad

The Strange Tale of Hector & Hannah Crowe
Nathaniel Hensley
ISBN: 978-1-937240-49-3
Genre: Young Adult
Available in paperback and eBook

Hector and Hannah Crowe are no strangers to the bizarre and supernatural. Ghosts, ghouls, mad scientists and revenants come with the territory when you are the children of the world's foremost paranormal investigators. The Crowes live in Strange Manor, the most haunted house in the most haunted little town in America, in the middle of a deep dark wood filled with mysterious beasts.

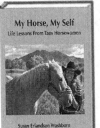

My Horse, My Self: Life Lessons from Taos Horsewomen
Susan Erlandson Washburn
ISBN: 978-1-937240-40-0
Genre: Equestrian Healing
Available in paperback and eBook

My Horse, My Self: Life Lessons from Taos Horsewomen is a collection of intimate interviews with eighteen passionate and self-reliant horsewomen living in Northern New Mexico. Speaking from the heart, they describe the ways their horses have sustained them through trauma, forced them to discover strengths---and weaknesses---they didn't know they had, and helped them develop the confidence to become more truly themselves. The interviews are accompanied by photographic portraits that convey the essence of each woman's story and depict the stark beauty of Taos' high desert surroundings.

All I Can Gather & Give
Patti Tana
ISBN: 978-1-937240-45-5
Genre: Poetry
Available in paperback and eBook

All I Can Gather & Give is a book of seventy-five poems by Patti Tana that is composed of three sections: "The Ally You Have Chosen," "Imperfect Circles," and "Every Season Has Its Beauty." This ninth collection of poems is a tribute to the poet's sources of inspiration in nature and the people she loves. In a voice intimate and accessible, Tana finds words to transcend adversity and affirm a life that is passionately lived.

Made in the USA
San Bernardino, CA
06 June 2015